Reflection

Book 1 — The Uishanole

Jordan T. Lefaivre

"There are two ways of spreading the light: to be the candle or the mirror that reflects it."

-Edith Warton

Chapter 1

Phoebe splashes cold water on her face and glances up at her reflection in the mirror. The girls' bathroom is unusually quiet for a change, which gives her an unexpected opportunity to compose herself. She runs her damp fingertips through her thick bangs and waist-length auburn hair, then rubs them over her thinly plucked eyebrows. Her skin is pale, with freckles scattered across her nose and if it weren't for her mismatching eyes—one blue right eye, the other brown—her face would be pretty unremarkable. Just an ordinary girl with an ordinary face. She adjusts the hem of her violet T-shirt, which is covered in a galaxy print, making sure to cover the waistband of her dark green skirt perfectly. Crouching, Phoebe yanks up her black socks and carefully tightens a loose shoelace on her purple-hued shoes. Standing up again, she re-adjusts her rectangular-shaped glasses and stares at her reflection one more time. A frown causes small creases to appear on her forehead as she discovers that the clasp of her necklace has once again slipped down to rest beside the pendant. She gives a gentle tug to reposition it to the back of her neck where it belongs.

Phoebe's pendant holds seven amethysts fused onto a thin metallic blue chain. Six smaller crystal spheres encircle the seventh amethyst, which is carved into the shape of a droplet. There are a number of reasons why this pendant is special: the seven violet crystals represent the age she was when her parents gave it to her on her birthday; the amethysts themselves are significant because they also feed her fascination for all things crystalline and most importantly, the pendant is a permanent reminder of her parents' love. She can't remember ever taking it off.

Satisfied that everything is in place, Phoebe emerges from the bathroom into the bustling white and red streaked halls of Ryerville High School. Her first period of the day, Music class, has left her feeling slightly giddy. After so many years of being home-schooled, she still isn't used to the compliments she continues to receive from her music teacher and fellow classmates. When it comes to music, especially the drums and cymbals, she has a natural sense of rhythm and finds it difficult to explain this to everyone else. With second period about to start, Phoebe realizes she spent more time in the bathroom than she had intended to. Keeping to the edges of the crowded hallways, she maneuvers through the maze of students towards her locker.

The first bell rings, notifying everyone to be at their next class before the second bell. Most of the students quickly rush into their classrooms. Their absence creates a void in the hallways. Phoebe finds the extra space comforting, since she has difficulty tolerating large crowds. Hurriedly turning the combination on her lock, she opens her locker door. A tidy pile of textbooks, a gym bag and her black backpack littered with pins of birds, cats, gems and flowers can be seen inside. She snatches her Grammar textbook for English class and a book her parents had purchased in an attempt to comprehend how Phoebe's mind works.

A loud bang echoes down the hallway.

Startled by the loudness, all of the remaining students, Phoebe included, turn their heads.

No...

A garbage can rolls on its side and five menacing figures appear at the end of the hall. *Mitch and his gang!* Mitch and his gang of bullies have ruled the school since the first day they walked through its front doors four years ago. Although they're all in the 12th grade, they should have graduated last year. Unfortunately for Phoebe and the rest of the student population, all five were held back due to poor grades.

As many of the students make the intelligent decision to power-walk to their classes, Mitch and his colleagues strut menacingly down the hallway towards her. Mitch's spiked black hair, along with his ripped black leather pants; make him look like he belongs onstage—similar to the front man of a heavy metal rock band. She can see the curled tail of his snake tattoo sneaking out from the cuff of his T-shirt. The rest of the gang could just as easily belong to the same band. Zack, who considers himself to be Mitch's right-hand man, has shaggy brown hair and wears a pair of black Levi's that look as if they've been retrieved from the bottom of a laundry hamper. Jill, the oldest of the group, wears her long blonde hair in greasy strands and uses dark black eyeliner to emphasize the blackness of her eyebrows. Brett, who's the joker in this deck of cards, sports a blonde Mohawk, has piercings jutting from his eyebrows, his lips and his ears. Amanda, the youngest of the group, has red wavy hair. She always seems to overdo it with the make-up she wears. Phoebe can't understand why they haven't been expelled.

One boy from her English class chooses that exact moment to walk out of his History class, providing a momentary distraction for the bullies.

Mitch grabs him by the arm and shoves him into one of the lockers.

"I assume a dwarf like you would have something for me?" Mitch mocks.

Phoebe's classmate struggles as he tries to free himself from Mitch's grasp, but he eventually gives up and hands over his backpack for inspection.

"What? No BLT sandwich today? You certainly are a disappointment."

Finding nothing of value, Mitch dumps the backpack contents onto the floor, leaving the boy to clean up the mess.

Phoebe cringes as she watches Mitch and his cronies move closer, wishing she had sped to class instead of gawking at them with apprehension. She feels paralyzed and finds herself unable to run.

Jill is the first of the group to reach her.

"Hey Pheebs…Talk to me," Jill teases.

Trying her best to ignore the bully, Phoebe turns her attention back to her locker.

"When *she* talks, *you* listen Dweebee," Zack commands.

"As if she's worth talking to. She couldn't even speak if all of humanity depended on it," Mitch sneers, looking down at her. "But at least try to tell us this Dweebee: why do you make yourself such a target? Little autistic freak, you're just begging to get jumped. Look at you, you don't do or say anything. You just stand there! What's wrong with you?"

Phoebe's head droops down. Her tormenters cackle. She continues trying her absolute best to ignore them and not cry or run away from school again. As insulting as they are, they are undeniably right about her having autism. Diagnosed with autism when she was three, Phoebe has always found it difficult to socialize with others, think abstractly and use proper language skills. Her autism is also the reason why she's sensitive to loud noises. Not only does everything sound louder to her, but she finds it extremely difficult to separate out what someone is saying to her from the background noise of daily life. It's overwhelming for her to take it all in. Although she finds that her autism gives her the ability to experience the world from a very different perspective, she wishes things were easier for her. The simplest of human interactions—eye contact, hand-holding and talking to unfamiliar people— are a challenge for her. As a result, she's become extremely shy and self-conscious and tends to keep her distance from anyone she doesn't know or anyone who's mean to her, like the school bullies. She also feels very tense about conversing with others, especially with people of the opposite gender. Phoebe fears that her autism will trigger her to act foolishly in front of them, something that has happened frequently in the past. Therefore, she tries her best to fit in by blending into the background. However, being autistic does provide her with a few advantages: high-level math skills, extreme attention to detail, impeccable timing and strong determination. People with autism can experience life more intensely and with the way her autism functions, she imagines it's comparable to an uneven scale. While Phoebe envisions scales of normal functioning people to be generally even or near-even, she pictures her own scale and those of other autistics to have the heavy side weighed down by their autisms' disadvantages, while the light side is lifted up by their autisms' unique gifts. The most fascinating thing about autism: every person diagnosed with it is different and unique in their own way.

"How about now, Dweebee? Got anything to say now?" Mitch asks.

Unable to say anything due to the fear-induced lump in her throat, Phoebe inspects the contents of her locker. Eyeing her plastic pencil case, she places her right hand on top of it. A very un-Phoebe like idea begins to formulate in her mind. From previous encounters with Mitch, she has learned that fighting back or telling on them are the two worst things she can do, but right now, they're hurting her so much, she can hardly resist doing nothing to make them stop.

"You know, I saw her freak out when a person with a dog passed by her last week," Amanda, who lives down the road from Phoebe, points out. "It wouldn't surprise me if she was afraid of a little Chihuahua."

"Aw, poor little girl," Brett says pitifully. "If a teeny tiny dog can scare her, then my appearance must be terrifying." He raises his hands like a monster, sticks out his pierced tongue and roars at Phoebe, making her cringe.

The gang laughs. She pulls her pencil case out of her locker and grasps it tightly.

"Well, if you're not going to talk, then give us something good!" Mitch orders. He looks at the necklace around her neck. "Say…What have you got around your neck? It looks expensive!"

Phoebe is starting to get really upset. This necklace is her most valuable possession, so it's usually hidden in her skirt pocket from the intimidators, but today she forgot to conceal it. She wields her pencil case like a sword as she tries to mentally prepare herself for what is about to happen next, while trying to not escalate the situation.

"Well, give it to us already!" Mitch shouts.

The second school bell resonates throughout the hall.

Phoebe turns around and pitches the pencil case at Mitch's face. There's stunned silence as the pencil case falls to the floor. Her pencils tumble out, skittering across the floor.

"My eye!"

Mitch clutches his face as he angrily attempts to grasp Phoebe's arm, his snarling voice filling the hallway. The commotion finally draws the attention of Phoebe's History teacher. He leans his head out of his classroom door.

"Hey! What's going on out here?!"

Surveying the scene, the teacher comes to a quick conclusion.

"Mitch, are you responsible for this?"

"Not me, man, why don't you ask her?" He points towards Phoebe.

The teacher looks at Phoebe. "Phoebe, did you do this?"

The reality of what she's done is finally catching up with her. The adrenaline slowly subsides. She blushes, her red face reminiscent of a sunburn, and is unable look the teacher or anyone else in the face. They're all judging her. She can feel every stare and it's intolerable.

Stop judging me!

She drops her books on the floor, turns and runs. Her locker door hangs open.

"Phoebe, wait! Please come back! We need to talk about this!"

Choking down her tears, Phoebe continues down the hallway and collides with her Educational Assistant, who has come looking for her.

"Phoebe, what's the matter?" she says.

Pushing past her very surprised E.A., Phoebe runs out the door that leads into the back fields of the school. The door creaks noisily and slams shut behind her. She sprints across the grass, and a few moments later she hears both the teacher and E.A. calling her name as they try to catch up. The consequences for fighting at Ryerville are pretty stiff and even though this fight was by no means Phoebe's fault, she's pretty sure she will somehow be blamed for what happened. Mitch and his friends seem to be able to talk their way out of any situation. She can already imagine just what type of story they've made up to tell the principal.

Panting heavily and wiping away the tears that continue to stream down her cheeks, she comes to a halt in an attempt to catch her breath. *Mom, Dad, please don't be hard on me for this! None of it was my fault!* Looking back, she's surprised to see how far she has run. With her shoes crunching on the gravel pathway leading up to the back entrance, Phoebe gradually moves towards the open back gate.

The rosebushes and other flowering shrubs making up the orderly paths of Ryerville's back garden now stand between her and the school. She glances over at the 11th grade students playing floor hockey in one of the large outdoor areas of the grounds. She gazes back behind her at the brightly coloured red brick walls of the school, which is a sharp contrast to the greenish red new leaves of the maple trees, the pink blossoms of the cherry trees and the mauve hues of the heather that line the pathway. A large decision now looms before her: should she go back and accept the consequences of her fight with Mitch or should she continue through the gate and go home?

I really don't want to ever go back to school after what happened. There is nothing left there for me and none of my classmates seem to want to help me. I just wish that Mom and Dad would let me be homeschooled again. Heaving a big sigh, Phoebe pushes her way through the gate. She strolls down the sidewalk of one of the busy streets of Vancouver, leading back to her nearby neighbourhood, trying her best to hide her tears so as not to attract any unwanted attention, wishing for something good to happen to make up for her rough day.

Chapter 2

The long, arduous day gives way to the dark coating of night. Only an hour earlier Phoebe had watched the most spectacular sunset. As the sun sinks sluggishly below the horizon, deep red and orange fingers stretch out to ensnare the clouds, giving them a pinkish hue that clashes with the remaining blue of the sky. A sudden storm has blown in from the Strait of Georgia. The wind howls angrily as it slams its full fury against the outside walls of her home, desperately trying to find a way to get inside. Rain mixed with hail pounds incessantly against Phoebe's window. Bright sky slashes of lightning, accompanied by disturbingly close claps of thunder, illuminate the night. It's definitely not a good night to be outside.

Phoebe sits at her bedroom desk with her laptop, playing her favourite song—'Stand Back' by Stevie Nicks—to help keep her outlook positive, in front of her trying to complete an assignment for her History class. She tries to ignore the resurfacing memories from earlier as she types studiously. But she can't concentrate. Phoebe turns her focus away from her computer and gazes around her room, lip-syncing to the music and smiling in appreciation at the many items designed to downsize her stress levels. The mauve walls are covered with small posters of birds and outer space, two of Phoebe's favourite interests. Stuffed animals sprawl in a row along her dresser, a 3D model of the solar system hangs above her bed and a collection of stone minerals juts from the top shelf above her computer desk. Her laptop sits in the centre of the desk next to a shelf filled with video games. Her music box features a fragile glass hummingbird hovering over a flower. She has a bookshelf crammed with well-loved books.

Unable to diminish her stress levels, Phoebe glances over at her orange tabby kitten, named Mysty (for Mysterious). As an only child, Phoebe has always longed for some form of companionship, but her social awkwardness makes it difficult to find friends. She originally wanted a bird, but due to her mom's allergies she had to make a compromise. It was decided she should get a kitten instead. Mysty was seen as the perfect solution: someone she can talk to who won't prejudge her. She's batting around an empty toilet paper roll, completely oblivious to the storm raging locomotive-like outside.

BOOM!!!

Thunder shakes the house. The storm must be right overhead. Cowering in fear, Mysty disappears under the bed. Her protruding tail has fluffed to twice its normal size. As another furious clap of thunder assaults the house, Phoebe covers her ears. *If this storm gets any louder, I'm joining Mysty under the bed.* Unblocking her ears, soft knocking on her bedroom door causes her to jerk. Her stress levels, already heightened because of the events at school, are really working overtime tonight because of the storm. Dreading the coming conversation with her parents, Phoebe waits for several seconds before giving them permission to come into her room. She stops the music and shuts her laptop. "Come in."

Pushing the door open, Phoebe's dad leans casually against the doorframe. The sheen of sweat on his arms and damp short brown hair indicates he has just finished a quick workout on the treadmill. Her mom comes quietly into the room and sits on the faded patchwork quilt that lies neatly folded at the foot of Phoebes' bed. She loosens her ponytail of long straight blonde hair and glances at Phoebe, pushing up her rectangular black framed glasses. Phoebe can see a look of concern reflected in her blue eyes. Her red hands and the citrusy smell of lemon dish soap indicate she has just finished the dishes. Phoebe feels a small twinge of guilt, since it was supposed to be her turn to help wash the dishes tonight.

Refusing to look at her parents, Phoebe absentmindedly spins the model solar system sitting on her desk. She knows from the way her parents entered the room that this won't be a pleasant conversation.

"We need to have a talk about what happened today," her dad says. His deep, gravelly Australian accented voice is tinged with concern and something else Phoebe can't quite place. Regret that he wasn't there to protect her, perhaps? She had long ago accepted the fact that his busy dental practice prevented him from spending more time with her.

"Okay," Phoebe gives the solar system a rather rough spin, causing the planets to wobble erratically on their axes. She drums her fingers rhythmically on the desktop.

Getting up from the bed, her mom walks over and takes the wildly spinning model away. She places it on the shelf above the desk, beside a framed picture of a young Phoebe wearing a big red bow in her hair.

"I told you not to perseverate with your items," she reminds Phoebe.

"Sorry," Phoebe apologizes still drumming her fingers on the desk, "it's just that I'm so…frustrated." Her dad pulls her into a bone crushing hug and whispers words of comfort in her ear. She feels safe in his embrace and desperately wishes she could stay like this forever.

"Why don't we all go sit down on the bed?" her mother's crisp British accent emphasizes the seriousness of the situation.

Phoebe picks a place right in the middle of her bed. She watches as her parents try to find comfortable positions on either side of her, settling in. She grabs her favourite stuffed penguin, worn and faded from all the love that has been lavished on it, and hugs it to her chest.

Her mom turns to look at her. "I just got off the phone with your principal."

"Really?" Phoebe hadn't even heard the phone ring over the noise of the storm.

"Yes. She reassured me that Mitch and his friends will be given a five-day suspension. She's also trying to convince the school board they should be expelled, if they misbehave one more time." Phoebe looks up at her mother's face and notes the deep worry lines on her forehead.

"Good, I hope they do get expelled," Phoebe mutters.

"What was that?"

"Oh nothing, mom." Phoebe turns her head. She can't stand seeing the look of betrayal in her mom's eyes.

"Phoebe, look at me. This is a very serious matter and I need you to pay attention."

Turning her head back, she's surprised to see there are tears in her eyes.

"Your principal also confirmed your punishment as well."

"And?"

Sighing heavily, her mother pauses. "You will receive five days of after-school detention."

"What?! No!" Phoebe can't believe what she's hearing. She has <u>never, ever,</u> had detention before in her entire life! In fact, she has rarely been punished at all, even at home!

"True…," her dad says. "It was very wrong of Mitch and his friends to do what they did, but that doesn't give you the right to hurt him in return. You attacked a known bully, although you acted in self-defense, and that made the situation worse. You have made an enemy out of Mitch and I can guarantee you things will escalate from here on in." With the concern deepening in his voice, Phoebe looks up at him, sighting the regret written all over his face. "I think it's good that you were able to fight back this time and I understand you were only trying to prevent them from taking your necklace. It shows how much you've grown since we've stopped home-schooling you. But, please don't make a habit of fighting your battles by yourself, let alone running away from school when the school day isn't finished yet. There's nothing wrong with going to a teacher or at least letting your E.A. know what's going on. That way you will know you have people ready to back you up."

"I'm so sorry." The tears she's been keeping in cascade down her cheeks. Wet drips land on her forearms. "I never meant to hurt you or mom. It all sort of just…happened."

Her mom wordlessly hands her the box of tissues.

Phoebe's dad rests his hand on her shoulder, gives it a comforting squeeze. She can feel his strength radiating down through her arm. Not to be outdone, Mysty abandons her hiding place under the bed and climbs up the bedspread onto Phoebe's lap. The roughness of her tongue feels like sand paper as she licks the palm of Phoebe's hand. Her loud purr vibrates against Phoebe's legs.

But it's not over yet. Hoisting Mysty off her lap, Phoebe clambers off of the bed and places her gently onto the ground. "I want, no, I NEED to go back to home schooling again!" She stamps her foot, causing Mysty to retreat. The kitten, being a relative newcomer to the household, is still young enough that she isn't accustomed to Phoebe's outbursts.

"Phoebe Laelynn Jordan!" her dad yells, stealing Phoebe's spotlight. "You can't live the rest of your life like a hermit! Cutting yourself off from the outside world is not the solution to this problem. I know this is difficult for you, but things will get better. I'm sure of it. You need to have a little faith in yourself. Besides, how do you expect to learn to live with your autism if you don't put yourself in situations beyond your control? All you have to do is gain some hope in life." He looks down at her and Phoebe can tell by the stormy colour of his brown eyes this is not the time to argue with him.

Phoebe blows her nose noisily with a tissue. Her eyes feel as if they have sand in them. She can feel the stickiness of tear tracks on her cheeks.

"Like me, your mother and the rest of our family have always said…even a speck of hope can take you a long way," her dad says.

Looking down at her lap, Phoebe refuses to even make an attempt at a response.

"I believe in you for finding the speck of hope Phoebe," her dad continues. "Remember, you are <u>The Bright and Shining Flower of Hope</u> just waiting to bloom. All you have to do is keep trying to make it blossom."

Phoebe's given title <u>The Bright and Shining Flower of Hope</u> are her first and middle name's meanings combined. The definition for Phoebe is "Bright, Shining" and for Laelynn is "Flower of Hope". As happy as Phoebe is with her names, she feels her inner Bright and Shining Flower of Hope hasn't even sprouted yet, no matter how hard she tries.

As Phoebe remains hushed, a silent message passes between her parents as they gaze at each other.

"How about this?" her mom says. "We would like you to at least try to make it through the rest of this school year and if it still doesn't work out, then we can think about going back to homeschooling, but I feel you won't be doing yourself any favours if you do end up going back."

"I guess I don't have a choice, do I?" Phoebe crosses her arms, sniffling. She knows this is one argument she won't be able to win. Sighing heavily, she turns to look to the roiling storm swirling outside her window.

"Get some rest and think about what we've talked about. Hopefully you'll be able to put this all into perspective in the morning." Her dad stands up and gives her shoulder one last squeeze. She doesn't look up, continuing to scowl out the window.

"Well, goodnight honey," her mom brushes a hand reassuringly against Phoebe's cheek and plants a quick kiss on the top of her head. "I'm really proud of you for making it through two-thirds of the school year."

"Have a nice sleep with pleasant dreams Phoebe-dee," her dad says.

As her parents head out, her mom hesitates and her dad pauses after her, glancing at her. She affectionately gazes back at Phoebe.

"Phoebe," her mom says. "We completely understand how much you wish to be 'normal', like your father and I." Phoebe stares gloomily at her. "But I'm afraid…autism isn't something that can possibly be removed." Phoebe's head droops down, but her mom steps towards her and gently lifts her chin up, helping her focus back on her. "But that doesn't mean it's impossible for you to have a happy life, just like my parents always taught me. Like everyone else, you can't always get what you want in life, but you can still find true happiness. I'm very confident that you'll find true happiness and your father and I are committed to help you find it."

Phoebe smiles, holding her mom's hand.

"Honora is right," her dad says. "And Phoebe, we truly love you the way you are and we wouldn't want you any other way because you are extraordinary."

"Thank you," Phoebe says.

"We love you immensely dear," her mom says and kisses Phoebe's cheek.

"I love you too."

"Thank you. Goodnight."

Slowly ushering her mom out of the room, her dad turns out the light before closing the door. The room is now completely dark. The only source of light is the continuing flashes of lightening from the storm outside. Each flash illuminates the room for mere seconds, but it's enough for Phoebe to make out the shadowy figures of the furniture in her room.

Phoebe smirks mischievously, reaching and opening her dresser drawer. She lifts her shirts up, revealing a sealed chocolate bar.

"Ace," Phoebe whispers. The word 'ace' is her way of expressing herself when she feels a positive emotion.

At least chocolate always makes me feel wonderful.

"And Phoebe, no eating chocolate this late," her mom says through the door.

SHOOT! CRAPEDY! CRAPEDY! CRAP! CRAP! Phoebe sighs in frustration, setting her clothing back on top of her chocolate and shutting the drawer.

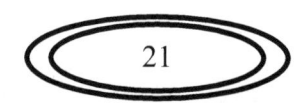

Using the flashes of light as a guide, Phoebe quietly makes her way towards the door. Placing her ear against the door, she listens for any hint of a sound from the other side. Hearing nothing, she slowly opens the door and winces as she waits for the squeal of un-oiled hinges. Nothing. Her father must've finally made good on his promise to oil them. "Please stay in my room Mysty." Sneaking silently down the hallway, she carefully places each footstep to avoid the squeaky floorboards. Finally reaching the top of the stairs, she peers down through the bars of the bannister into the living room below. Her parents sit facing the fireplace, cuddled on the sofa. Straining her ears, she can make out their conversation.

"I hope Phoebe realizes we're only trying to do what's best for her," her mother says, gazing into the comforting orange flames.

"Don't worry," her dad says, "she just needs time for all of this to sink in. It's a new experience for her. After being homeschooled and tutored for so long, she doesn't realize how important it is to have her own friends, especially around her own age. I have a feeling that if she can get through to the end of the school year, she'll have at least one new friend. Maybe it will even be that boy William she's always talking about from her English class."

"You're probably right, but it makes me very sad to see her leaving for school every single day with that haunted look on her face. I can't help but worry about her."

"I know. I worry about her too, but she just has to understand that this is how life is and that this is the best that we can do for her. Besides, her communication skills have improved a lot with all the tutoring. Deep down I believe she's ready to be more involved with the public. Now it's mostly just a matter of facing her fears and overcoming her shyness. After all, her E.A. is there supporting her with her communication and education too, so it's not like she isn't getting help when needed."

"That's very true, but…I'd love to see her live life more happily."

"Me too." Phoebe's dad wraps his arm around her mom's shoulder. They rest their heads against each other.

"How can we ever be happy, when she is never happy?"

"I don't know."

Saddened, Phoebe quietly walks back to her room. She can't believe the conversation she overheard.

"Great," Phoebe says, "so as long as I'm never happy, my parents can't ever be happy. If I keep this up, I'll be an even bigger burden to them than I already am."

Phoebe has always felt her autism has also made her parents' lives way more difficult than just hers, which she can't help but feel guilty about. She hums her favourite song to calm herself. As pressuring as attending a public school is for her, she feels she should begin forcing herself to take new approaches to try becoming more positive and independent for her parents' happiness. She does understand that they only want what's best for her, but given how much trouble she goes through to just fit in, is this really what's best for her? Is all their effort worth their time? Would she really be happier this way?

Mysty crawls up to her, meowing softly to soothe her. Phoebe picks her up and hugs her tightly. She kisses the top of her head before placing the kitten on the quilt at the foot of the bed. She wanders over to her window, checks the lock, seeing it's still rusted and jammed in the unlocked position since the last couple days. She sighs irritably. *Dad was able to oil my door's hinges yet he still couldn't make time to fix my lock again. Oh well. Thankfully this neighbourhood isn't known for its break-ins.*

Phoebe gropes her way to the head of her bed. Pulling down the covers, Phoebe slips into bed. She turns on the hummingbird music box sitting on her nightstand. Its soothing melody and Mysty's reassuring purrs help calm her. Being too weary, she doesn't even bother taking off her clothes, her necklace or her glasses. As the pulsating sound of thunder continues outside, she pulls her blankets up to her chin, getting comfortable in her bed. Mysty snuggles against her legs.

"You want to sleep with me tonight?" Phoebe asks.

Mysty yawns, closes her eyes and tucks her tail under her tiny paws. Phoebe smiles at her. "Love you too. Goodnight Mysty." Yawning deeply, Phoebe rolls over on her side and stares at the black nothingness of her bedroom wall. In the darkness, the posters on the wall are only dim outlines. Her eyelids feel heavier with each blink and her music box lulls her, slowly, into a deep sleep.

Lightning slices to the ground hours later, leaving the ground smoking and charred outside Phoebe's window, as the thunder picks up a cataclysmic intensity. The wind continues to batter furiously against the walls while Phoebe snores, Mysty curled close. There's a brief moment of quiet, and then suddenly it's as if the storm has released all of its stored up energy into one earth-shaking boom. Phoebe claws her way from the fog of unconsciousness, her dreams dissipating in a ghostly fog. She's still blinking sleep from her eyes when the curtain across the room draws her attention.

What the?!

As she watches, horrified, a red-skinned clawed hand emerges from the chaos of the storm. The window is half-open now—no wonder the volume of the thunder had escalated so abruptly—and gusts of ice-rain blow into her room, dampening the floor and blowing objects off her desk and shelves. Sniffing the air tentatively, a dark cloaked figure pokes its head into Phoebe's room. Without hesitating, Phoebe scoops up Mysty, making her meow in protest, and tucks both of them under her blanket. She shushes her kitten, silencing her, as she holds her in place. *It's only a nightmare! There's no way someone or something would have a hand like that in real life!*

Phoebe shuts her eyes firmly and fakes sleep. The figure swishes softly across her room and approaches her bedside, the rain and wind at its back. *It's only a dream and that's that!* She overhears what sounds like another set of footsteps quietly tiptoeing up to her bedside as well. *Was that another one?!* Phoebe opens up one eye a crack and sees two blurry figures through her thin sheet and blanket staring down at her. One is taller, the other shorter. She shuts her eye again. *Oh my gosh! There's two of them! I best scream to wake up my parents! NO! The burglars might shoot me if they know I'm awake and calling for help! Wait...the clawed hand...this is undeniably a dream. They'll go away soon enough. Calm down Phoebe.*

Now the darkness within her eyelids develops a shade of glowing orange light. *Now what's going on?*

She starts overhearing a man's formal voice whispering excitedly in an unfamiliar foreign language. *What?*

With her eyes still shut, Phoebe feels her blanket being tugged off her face. Her whole body goes rigid, knowing dreams can't physically pull blankets off of people. The orange glow brightens, making her clench her eyes even tighter. *Wait, THIS IS NO DREAM! THIS IS FOR REAL! WHAT DO I DO?!* Phoebe continues to pretend she's still asleep.

She hears an enthusiastic young boy's voice with a casual tone, murmuring the alien tongue too. As the two foreigners converse with one another, their tones begin to sound concerned and they pause for a few seconds. The orange glow diminishes to a much dimmer red glow and they proceed communicating, sounding even more worried. Being incapable of understanding them to overhear their intentions Phoebe's inner spirit panics. *What are they saying?! Why are they here?! What do they want from me?! What are they even?! I can't handle this anymore!*

Giving up all pretense of being asleep, Phoebe opens her eyes and is shocked to see the two shadowy figures in her room, both of whom now look stunned to see her awake. It's hard to make out who they are in the darkness, especially since they're in black cloaks, but she can tell by the shapes of their bodies that they aren't quite human. Even their eyes don't appear to be natural. Summoning the courage to scream for her parents, Phoebe begins to panic but the taller figure clamps a hand over her mouth before she can make a sound.

The adult being mutters to the young one with alarm, as Phoebe cringes from his touch, struggling to free herself from his grasp, twirling and flailing. Grabbing both ends of the blanket, they completely wrap it around her and Mysty, who yowls in panic. Phoebe screams, desperately hoping her parents will wake up, but knowing them, they wear earplugs while they sleep during a raucous storm. She's being hefted over the man's shoulder potato sack-like, and he moves towards the forceful winds buffeting the open window.

The older monster yells gibberish downwards.

Phoebe doesn't have time to scream before she can feel herself hurtling through the air. Her muscles tense with anticipation, but before she can collide with the ground she feels two thick arms cushion her, cradling her quivering body.

The one grasping her calls out in the unknown speech with a deeper man's voice.

She hears nearby branches scrabbling and cracking as her kidnappers clamber down the tree. *Who are these people?!*

The man's grasp is shaky now. His heavy breathing punctuates the pitter-patter of sprinting footsteps. Away from the sanctuary of her bedroom, the thunder sounds even more deafening. Shrieking winds blow roughly against her and torrential rain pours out of the sky, making the blanket cling tight against her skin. She watches her neighbours' houses pass by through a tiny hole in the blanket at her eye level that Mysty made a week ago. She can make out the distant city lights of Vancouver in the darkness.

I have to get attention, she thinks, before letting loose with her loudest, longest wail. Her shrieking triggers a chain reaction of flicked-on lights in the houses all along the block and a neighbourhood dog to bark. She feels her captors hesitate and hears them panic to one another. *My screaming is working!*

"H-Help! Help me!" Phoebe screams.

She struggles, watching as the ground gets further away, realizing they're ascending up a nearby tree. Soon enough they've reached a roof, and there's nothing she can do about it, except scream until rescuers come. Still carrying their precious cargo, the trio hastily leaps from one rooftop to the next, making their way towards the sanctuary of the woods. Phoebe lets her body go slack as the shock of what's happening begins to hit her. Blood trickles down her cheek where a branch tore at her, soaking into the sheet, and as they clatter across the slate tile roof of one building she thinks she can hear the scraping of claws. Coming to her neighbourhood's edge, she gazes at the lawn moving towards her, overhearing her captors climb down a tree. Reaching the ground, they resume sprinting away. Phoebe clutches Mysty against her chest as she watches Vancouver itself fade further into the distance, as the creaking dark of the deep forest surrounds them. She ceases calling out, seeing it's too late for anyone to hear her anymore.

Finally, once the houses are out of sight, the trio stops with a jolt. Phoebe tears the blanket's hole slightly wider and peeks through it. She catches a glimpse of their scaly skin and what looks like tails hidden underneath their long dark cloaks. *Who are these…gators?!*

The boy chatters with a sigh and the thinner man says a brief something, clutching a staff with a glowing red orb affixed to the top. Phoebe watches curiously as he holds it out. It glows luminously brighter as he waves it around in a circular pattern. A glowing whirlwind, filled with streams of colourful light mysteriously appears on the ground in front of him. Its appearance is so bright it absorbs all of the darkness in the surrounding area. Phoebe stares at it in astonishment. *Oh my gosh! Is that some kind of underground tornado?! But how?!* He lowers his staff to the underground cyclone, casting an orange magical beam. His spell gets sucked into the whirling magic, giving it an orange shade.

Without another word, the three beings leap simultaneously towards the vortex with the larger one clutching Phoebe and Mysty. Phoebe screams one more time.

Chapter 3

Phoebe wakes with a gasp. For a moment it feels like she's been turned into a statue. The glacial chill of the translucent surface has settled deep into her body. Her hip aches, her teeth chatter and she can feel the lingering effects of a headache. Her hazed surroundings are nearly impossible to make sense of in the dim light. Slowly the fog seems to lift, as she blinks, and her surroundings come into focus. Ignoring her skull-throbbing headache, Phoebe pushes herself into a sitting position. The last thing she can remember is turning off her bedroom light, crawling beneath the warm layers of the blankets on her bed and…getting kidnapped! *Wa-wait! I was being kidnapped! Where have they taken me?!*

A quick look at her surroundings is enough for her to come to the conclusion she's definitely not anywhere familiar. This place doesn't even come close to resembling anywhere she's ever been to or heard of in her entire life. Endless duplicates of herself cover the entire area, gazing out at her in astonishment.

"What the?!" Phoebe says, her voice echoing across the empty room.

Gritting her teeth, Phoebe stands to face her doppelgangers. They mimic her movements with unique precision. She carefully makes her way towards one of them and watches as all of the others head to the exact same place. Her head spasming with each step.

"Mirrors?" Phoebe says with her eyes widening with realization.

Looking into the mirror, she realizes every square inch of the walls is covered by mirrors of virtually every shape, size and description, especially their framing, without a single duplicate among them. Any space not occupied by mirrors has been overtaken by glowing colossal stained glass windows, allowing coloured light to filter into the room. The priceless detailing of the mirrored frames causes the light to glow as it's slowly absorbed back into the mirrors, but something even more extraordinary is happening. Phoebe finds herself captivated by colourful streams of light floating in the air. The shimmering reminds her of stardust or perhaps the Northern Lights. The brightly coloured motes of light reflect off of every surface. They seem to change colour every few seconds too. She's struck by their extreme beauty.

"Ace…What is all of this?"

Moving silently around the room, she discovers the area is more of a hallway than an actual room.

"Why would they bring me here?" She taps her foot on the solid floor only to have that one single step echo throughout the room. She examines the ground and comes to the conclusion that the floor is likely made out of something closely related to obsidian. The black volcanic glass creates a mirrored surface that reflects herself, the many lights and her reflected images on the mirrored walls. In fact, except for the mirrors and windows, everything appears to be made out of the same volcanic glass as the floor. She bends down and feels the floor. *Glassy stone material? Just what kind of a place is this?* She cranes her neck as she stares overhead. She's able to make out that even the incredibly high arched ceiling is covered with mirrors, all slightly bent, giving her the illusion of hundreds of shrunken Phoebes glancing curiously down at her. *What's with all these mirrors?*

She looks ahead, detecting a blue glow. Interested, she walks up to it, discovering its source is a finely crafted scepter resting on the floor. Its ink-black shaft is also made of obsidian, and a radiant blue crystal orb the size of a melon is set on top. Crouched on top of the orb is a black eagle-like creature with a severe beak and unforgiving, luminous crystal blue eyes. Wings outstretched, the bird grasps the orb tightly in its talons. *What is this?* She seizes the scepter and strokes the bird, tentatively, curiously. The scepter gives off an aura of power and it's extremely light. The orb's light reflects off the mirrors all over the room.

What is this thing? Where did it come from? Why are its eyes glowing…? Whatever it is, it would make a useful flashlight.

Phoebe takes a few hesitant steps forward, wondering if she's safe and where her kidnappers could be. She paces down the hallway as it curves off to the right. Following the turn, she enters into a grander passage with an obsidian stairway, more windows and mirrors and even statues reaching up to fifty feet in height. Some of the statues are human-like in appearance, while others look as if they have come out of someone's warped imagination. The mystical being sculptures have sharp teeth, claws and lizard-like tails. Like Phoebe, they're also holding up enormous stone scepters, only there are no birds or figurines on them. They look suspiciously like mythological monsters that would love to gobble up someone as small as Phoebe. She finds this immensely disturbing as she passes by, especially since they appear to be staring down at her as she passes. The streams of light seem to have a life of their own as they follow the mystifying maze. She shudders with the sensation of the labyrinth itself being alive.

Down one hallway, Phoebe reaches an area where there are several openings leading to both the right and the left. Each one appears to entice her to enter it. Making a quick decision, she journeys through the first opening on the right. Proceeding through it and down yet another hallway, Phoebe continues to admire the colourful streams of light, waving the scepter at them, causing them to spin around in the air. *I can imagine Mysty having a ball swatting at this light.*

A sudden worrisome thought flicks on in Phoebe's head.

"Mysty! Where are you?!" Phoebe calls ahead and behind, echoing down the passages. *Oh no! Mysty's gone! How could I have forgotten about her?! She could be anywhere in this oversized labyrinth! Unless, the kidnappers have her with them still or worse...maybe they ate her!* "No...not Mysty..." The sensation of losing her friend consumes her as she cries out. She gradually halts her sobbing after half a minute and concentrates, using her best efforts to problem solve. *But...I don't know for sure if they ate her or even have her. She could've just wandered off while I was unconscious. Maybe if I continue exploring, I may reunite with her.* Staring down her chosen pathway, she stands up high, wipes her tears away and paces forward down the aisle.

After quite some time, she enters into a massive room intersecting with the hallway she has been travelling down. Its ceiling is so far away, she can't even see it and just like every other area she's been to in this unusual place, mirrors cover the walls. Gigantic statues of mystical beings and creatures litter the room: each one becoming increasingly more bizarre and fantastical and all of them appearing to be suspended in time. Some of the statues look as if they are caught halfway through the walls. It's almost as if the walls grew around them. Phoebe finds the lifelike appearances of the statues extremely unnerving. She feels as if they've been awaiting her arrival.

"You're being silly," she scolds herself, "statues can't come to life." *Or can they?*

Dragging her attention away from the statues, Phoebe looks around the room. She's surrounded by dozens of zigzagging and spiraling staircases. Each staircase heads in a completely different direction from its closest neighbour.

I wonder which way I should go now. "Mysty!" Focusing only on her sense of hearing, she listens to her call's sound waves bouncing around the chamber without a hint of a mewing response. *It would be a lot easier to choose a path if I could hear Mysty calling from one of them.*

A shrieking noise nearly deafens her. Alarmed, she almost loses her grip on the scepter and, looking down, she sees the glowing blue eyes of the scepter's bird figurine glaring back at her. She drops it in shock and with an angry squawk the bird launches itself off of the orb and comes to rest on the intricately carved banisters. It looks back at her, motioning with its left wing, and even though she's sure something bad is probably going to happen, Phoebe picks up the scepter and decides to follow it.

"You want me to follow you?"

The bird nods and flies up towards the top of the staircase. Phoebe races up after it. Quickly finding herself out of breath, she wishes the cheeky little thing would slow down just a bit. Reaching the top, she enters another passage filled with mirrors, statues and stained glass windows.

This entire situation is getting out of hand. I really need to find Mysty and get out of here.

"Wait for me!"

Phoebe finally catches up to the bird, which is perched on one of the statues' folded arms. It chirps down at her and flies off, directly into an oval shaped mirror hanging on the wall where the hallway ends and another intersects, disappearing into its depths. Stunned, Phoebe watches in amazement as the mirror begins to glow. *This whole place is becoming stranger and stranger.* As she gets closer to the mirror, an odd reflection coalesces inside of it, separating itself from all the other reflections. Gazing into the mirror, she's surprised to see an image of a young girl holding the exact same scepter she has. She squints at the image: the girl in the mirror has similar features to Phoebe, yet at the same time there are enough differences to confirm that this is not her true reflection. Although the figure in the mirror could probably pass herself off as Phoebe's twin, there are enough subtle differences between them—the biggest one being that her reflection doesn't seem to be human. A crystal crown rests gracefully on top of her long, navy blue hair. Her white silk gloves and glistening teal gown contrast against the blue of her skin, the violet hue of her neck and her sharp fine thin navy blue eyebrows. She looks reptilian, and whereas Phoebe has one blue eye and one brown eye, her reflection's irises are purple. The sclera of her eyes are not even white, but instead a deep emerald. They appear to be roughly the same age, but overall the sight of this mirrored person astounds Phoebe so much she cannot get her tongue to work.

She glances back, trying to spot the girl, but it's clear Phoebe's the only one there. She stares back at the reflection with a sense of panic, trying to put the logical pieces together. If this is a reflection, then who and where is this girl?

Who is this person?

As she watches, the girl raises her arm, making Phoebe gasp and back away three steps. The girl gestures for her to come forward and Phoebe points, hesitantly, at herself. The girl nods her head and slowly fades, almost as if she's evaporating.

"Wait!" Phoebe calls out, but it's too late. Her own reflection reappears. Gazing at herself in the mirror, she wonders why the girl would signal for her to come forward. She reaches out and touches the mirror, lightly, with the tips of her fingers. Before she can shriek, she's absorbed into the mirror, and as she blinks in shock, she finds herself in a vast room with streams of light blurring the distant walls. A gorgeously bright amber-white crystal chandelier dangles, casting dancing light across the red marble floor. She can hear people moving, concealed by the foggy streams of light, talking formally, as if she's stumbled into a mansion party.

Ace!

A squawk breaks Phoebe's attention, and she pivots to see where the noise is coming from. The bird statue unfurls one wing and motions for her to follow.

"It's you again," Phoebe says, approaching it. "What's going on here?"

The bird motions with its beak in the direction of the girl from the mirror, who emerges from the streams of light. Without a doubt it's the girl from the mirror, except she appears the way Phoebe looked six years ago. For a moment Phoebe forgets about being kidnapped, about waking up in a mirrored maze and about the strange bird perched next to her. Her doppelgänger is wearing a stunning purple dress with gems sewn into the fabric, her tiara's diamonds sparkling. She's chatting with indistinct mystical beings covered by the light streams.

"I just love your dress, Your Highness," a woman says.

She's royalty?

"Thank you very much," the girl formally replies with the same voice Phoebe had at her age. "I had this dress made especially for tonight."

"You have crystals sewn into your dress, and many more gifts await you," a man says. "Don't you feel concerned about growing spoiled?"

"Well," the girl says, chuckling. "Maybe just a little. I've been working lately on cutting back."

In the distance Phoebe hears a young boy's voice. He's behind Phoebe, within the swirling clouds of light, approaching a magical-looking banquet table. The girl turns to look in that direction, and Phoebe follows her gaze.

"Yether cakes! Yether cakes!" he yells excitedly.

The girl becomes agitated, rocking from one foot to the other in agitation. She grabs hold of her tiara and sprints through the shimmering crowd, startling the ghostly guests and charging in the direction of the boy.

"You stay away from those!" she yells. "Get away!"

As she runs, a lizard-like tail snakes from the bottom of her dress swinging back and forth. It's blue with violet skin underneath, and Phoebe realizes with a start that all the other people are sporting tails too. *What kind of species is this?!* She's still thinking about that when her clone turns and races towards her. She backs away, startled, but before she can get out of the way the girl swishes through her body and remerges on the other side.

What's going on?! Is...none of this real? Was that a hologram?

The girl trips over a chair, catching herself by performing an incredibly agile somersault and speeds towards the boy. She wrenches a plate of frosted bun-like cakes from his grip.

"Please pardon my vulgar side," the girl announces, "but you all know it tortures me to share my yether cakes!"

Phoebe's startled by the princess' behaviour, but is reminded of her own relationship to chocolate. She glances at the bird statue, wondering how any of this could be real. *Am I dreaming or is this reality? All of this feels real, but...* She thinks of past dreams, how realistic they seemed, and wonders if perhaps that's what's going on. But before she can formulate a question, the bird is spreading its wings again, swirling up a tornado of rainbow-streaked light. Around her, the princess, the boy and everyone else fade.

When the light streams settle, Phoebe finds herself in a new room. She brushes her wind-swept hair out of her face and gazes around a grand, darkened royal chamber. She can faintly make out a vast marble desk with an enormous oval-shaped mirror above it. There are fine cushions piled everywhere, and nearby there's an open chest stuffed with toys in the likeness of mystical beings and animals. There's a massive wooden wardrobe, many arched windows with green drapes, and finely carved stone walls with elaborate designs. Another gleaming chandelier, this one with purple gleaming crystals hangs down from the ceiling. The nightstands beside the King-sized bed each have a luminous purple crystal lamp that illuminates the rosy-hued bedspreads. Pink silk curtains are tied back on the mahogany bedposts.

Phoebe spots the royal girl, seeming to be twelve years old, lying on the bed, holding a glowing crystal the size of a tennis ball. Nearby there are two lizard creatures snoozing on the tiled ground. They look like Komodo Dragons with aqua-coloured skin and pebbled yellow bellies. Unexpectedly, a creaking noise oozes out from behind one of the curtains. The princess drops the gem and stares at the window. Phoebe feels afraid for her, guessing someone or something must be trying to break into the princess' room, like what she herself had gone through not too long ago. Her pets wake up and hiss, baring their pointed teeth. The princess immediately shushes them.

"Kuzy! Motis!" she whispers. "Pretend to sleep and don't make any movements or sounds right now! Trust me, I have a plan!" Her pets lay their heads back down. *What in the world is she doing?! Call for help or something!* The princess opens one of her night stands' shelves, tosses her book and crystal into the drawer, and then shuts it. She pulls a smoothly carved green scepter, similar to the one Phoebe's currently holding but with a yellow orb, from beneath her bed. She hastily tucks both herself and the scepter under the blankets, hiding its glow. The curtains slowly part, revealing a massive figure, and even though she can't make out the monster's appearance, his size is enough to frighten her. A low, growling exhale accompanies each step. He holds out a dagger, the only part of him not blocked by the shimmering streams of light, and aims it at the princess' chest.

With her eyes still shut, the princess thrusts the scepter up through the blanket. A bright blue beam bursts forth with a loud blast. The force hurls the blankets entirely off of the bed, draping them over the monster. Its power sends him crashing into the wooden wardrobe and knocks the dagger from his grip. He collapses to the ground, motionless, and the princess' pets approach the failed assassin growling ferociously. A crowd barges through the open door, surrounding the fallen hulk.

"An intruder! He was trying to murder the princess!"

"Fetch the king and queen immediately!"

"Why didn't you call for help?!"

The princess waves her hand. Immediately they're silent. "I'm completely fine. I figured I could take that assassin down by lowering his guard and pretending to be asleep so that he would come close enough to attack. Besides, if I called for help, he probably would've heard me and pitched that dagger right at me from the other side of the room."

Phoebe stares at the royal in astonishment. Phoebe would've panicked and screamed for help, but the princess bravely stayed put and defended herself like a warrior.

Oh my gosh...she straight up defeated that killer without backup! She's unbelievably brave to face someone or...something as huge as that! I bet she could stand up to any bully that gets in her way.

The bird whistles, making the light-streams fluctuate. Phoebe blinks her eyes curiously as the room around her disappears. Suddenly large crowds of shaded figures surround her, applauding. She stands on a hefty green crystal platform as it moves down the white-bricked street of a town. She's surrounded by smooth red ribbon with blue and yellow octagonal and diamond shaped gems sewn into it. There's a massive silk tarp above made of the same material overhead. Multi-coloured confetti falls everywhere and beautiful fireworks, which are remarkably clear for the daytime, shoot to the skies from the neighbouring crowds.

Phoebe glances back. There are several shadowy figures standing guard on the platform too, in front of three crystal thrones. Everyone is blurred except the princess who happily waves at the crowds amassed on either side. This time she appears about ten, she's wearing a fine blue dress with purple and red streaks sewn into it, and she's wearing the tiara from earlier and other priceless-looking jewelry on her fingers and around her neck.

There's that princess. I must be in the front of a parade now. Well, I'm happy as long as no one can see me. Phoebe stares at her twin's jewelry with amazement, especially her necklace, containing vast red, orange, yellow and black oval gems. *Ohh...Those minerals are amazing.*

The princess turns to her right and stops grinning. Her expression becomes one of pity. Curious, Phoebe's eyes dart to follow her gaze. From what she can make out from beyond the blotchiness, there's a boy wearing torn clothing. He looks poor. Phoebe turns her focus back on the princess, who places her hand on her necklace. She glances down at it, and her eyes widen with awareness. She unclasps it and points away from the penniless character.

"Hey Mother! Father!" the princess says. "Look at that beautiful float over there!"

"Which one?" her mother asks, as everyone turns their heads to where the princess is directing them. With everyone, except Phoebe, distracted by the parade float, the princess pitches her necklace at the homeless figure. The needy boy catches her jewelry and jumps about in wonder. Phoebe watches her alien duplicate grin mischievously and wink.

That was very generous of her. I'd find it challenging to give up jewelry like that.

The princess innocently focuses back on her parents and guards, who are still looking for the parade float that caught her interest.

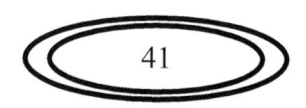

"Whoops, my mistake," the princess says. "I thought you could see it from here, I guess I was wrong."

Phoebe sighs. She glares down at the bird. "All right, you. This is neat, but I still don't understand what the purpose behind all this is. Can you please tell me what's going on? Is this a dream? Who is this girl and why does she look like me?"

The bird chirps, seemingly amused, then glides over to her scepter. It perches on the crystal orb with its wings open wide and slowly solidifies into its original position. Again the streams of light flow, whipping her hair across her face. And then, once again, she's in the mirror-filled halls.

"I'm back here again?" Getting impatient and frustrated at not knowing what's going on, Phoebe stamps her foot, which echoes down the halls. "Just what is this place?! Where am I?! Someone answer me!"

"**Phoebe…Phoebe…Phoebe…**," an eerie, very massive, smooth, super deep, echoey sounding voice begins chanting her name.

Petrified, Phoebe scans the darkness, looking for the voice's source. *Who or what was that?!* She stares back at the mirror, but the voice couldn't have been her reflection—the voice was obviously a man's.

"**Phoebe…Phoebe…Phoebe…**" The voice speaks louder and more insistently. It sounds sinister, snake-like, and malevolent. Then she hears echoing footsteps, giant booming thumps, and her eyes widen in fear. She panics, chooses a random hallway, then sprints away while the voice echoes loudly through the halls. Her flight is stopped short by the abrupt ending of the hallway. She finds herself in another cavern, this one filled with even more mirrors and statues of mystical creatures. Grasping the scepter tightly, she ducks under the belly of a vicious three-eyed creature that looks vaguely like a tiger. Up close it seems even more life-like than it did from far away. Every hair of its fur has been captured in exquisite detail. There are grooves in the floor, seemingly from its claws, as it has a wicked gleam in its eyes. She can almost imagine it breathing.

"Phoebe…Phoebe…Phoebe…"

Peering out into the room, she can see four gigantic black paws. The monster's claws click on the floor, echoing in the crypt-like stillness of the room. Phoebe trembles—she's always been afraid of dogs, but this escalates her fear of canines to a whole new level. *OH MY GOSH?! Why a giant canine?!* The room is plunged into absolute darkness. Phoebe crouches, covering her head with her hands for added protection. She can hear loud snuffling as it uses its monstrous snout to sniff out her hiding place.

"I can smell you," his voice echoes.

PLEASE GO AWAY!!!! If I really am dreaming, please wake up Phoebe! Please…wake…up!

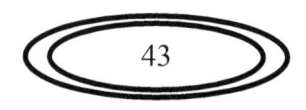

No such luck. The creature appears above her hiding place and, with a violent roar, wrenches the statue from the floor. It tumbles and cracks, crashing heavily into the wall of mirrors and sprinkling diamond-like shards of glass across the floor. Mini auroras suddenly arise from the destruction, filling the room and illuminating the creature looming over her: half-man, half-wolf, he's covered in smoky fur and has a taut club-like tail stretched out behind him. His pointed ears stand erect, bat-like, and his eyes contain black sclera, blood-red irises and deep black pupils shaped like nine-pointed stars. She can see dark auras, similar to the light-streams but dark red, encompassing him and his hot breath dampens her face. The creature grins down at her, showing off blade-like teeth, while saliva dribbles off its black tongue.

As the monster lunges at her, Phoebe emits a piercing scream and dives past its chin. As she slides along the ground she can feel his fur brush against her legs. Her chin bangs against the ground. The creature raises his head high, roaring out in frustration. Blinking away her tears, Phoebe scrambles to her feet and makes a run for it.

What do I do?! I can't hide from it! It will only smell me out again! She glances at the mirrors and eagerly gasps, forming a plan. *Hey! I can go into the mirrors to hide from it! Or...no! The monster just broke many mirrors! It could kill me by smashing the mirrors I'm within.* "Wake up! Wake up!"

The monster shoves massive lizard-like statues down, sending them crashing towards Phoebe, but luckily she just dodges them left to right. She jogs up and down the vast stairways and through numerous hallways and chambers without the creature even being winded. Then, reaching a staircase, she trips. Her elbow hits the ground hard and she crumples, crying out in pain, as the creature wraps its leathery wet tongue around her. For a moment she feels like a bug caught in a toad's grasp, but as he proceeds to lift her towards his mouth Phoebe screams, jabbing her scepter's pointed bottom into the roof of his mouth. He roars, dropping Phoebe back onto the stairs, then moans and slurps in pain. She watches for only a moment, covered in droplets of saliva, before scrambling up the stairs on all fours. But the exhaustion is catching up. The monster makes another lunge, and she escapes it, but how long can she keep doing this? Racing to the end of the passageway, Phoebe encounters an obsidian staircase with elaborately carved banisters. The staircase appears to ascend into emptiness. It's suspended over a bottomless chasm with mirrors aligned on every inch of its walls. *More stairs?!* She has no choice. As she takes the steps two at a time she can hear the monster crushing the railings behind her. Her thighs burn, her lungs feel ready to give out, and she's wondering how much longer she'll make it when suddenly she comes across a gap. The staircase had been caved in, and the higher steps are far out of her reach. Below her is nothing but bottomless chasm aligned with mirrors.

What do I do?! What do I do?! What do I do?!

Phoebe looks down at the scepter in her hand, the monster's thunderous approach making the ground tremble beneath her shoes. The orb is beginning to pulse, as if a white light is emerging from deep within it. She has no choice, she realizes, as cold wind swirls from the chasm. The cliff walls surrounding her are sheer and smooth, with no ledges or handholds. There's nothing beneath her but infinite depth, nothing behind her but certain death. She takes a deep breath, clenches her scepter tight, and hurls herself into the abyss.

Chapter 4

For a moment Phoebe forgets to be afraid. She hurtles past the sleek black walls surrounding her on all sides, and for a moment she feels almost weightless. Above her the monster roars from the stairs above, its echoing voice becoming increasingly faint. *How deep does this pit go?!* She's about to scream when the scepter's orb begins to glow orange, as if something's heating it from within. The orange transitions into a fiery yellow and finally to a blinding white that swallows everything.

Still shaking, Phoebe jolts up in bed and lets out a quick scream of alarm. Mysty, lying at her side, jumps.

"Mysty! You're here! Sorry I scared you," Phoebe says, relieved, patting the orange tabby on the head. Mysty glares at her, annoyed, but relaxes back against her side.

So everything that I thought was real was really just a dream after all. A very realistic, absurd one—First, I was kidnapped by those creepy men, and then I was in those mirrored caverns. And that's right! I came across someone who looks like me. Not to mention the monster. Looking around the room, she tries to make out the comforting shapes of her furniture, but everything is blurred. *Strange, I don't remember taking off my glasses.* She reaches over for the glasses which are usually on the nightstand beside her bed. They're not there. As a matter of fact, all she can feel is more bedding.

Blindly fumbling for her glasses, she creeps to the other side of the bed thinking she perhaps left them on her other nightstand, unusual as that might seem. *It feels as if my bed has doubled or even tripled in size. It...it even feels much softer than usual.* Finally reaching the edge of the mattress, she spies her glasses sitting on a dresser right next to the nightstand and puts them on. The blurred furniture immediately comes into focus: this is definitely not her room! The ceiling appears to be at least thirty feet high, with a beautiful blue crystal chandelier reflecting the light. The exquisitely carved walls and carpeting are decorated with swirling abstract designs. Framed pictures of fantastical creatures, none of which Phoebe recognizes from the many stories she has read, hang on the walls. The pale rose coloration of the marble floor is an exact match to the colours of the fine linen drapes which have been drawn back to allow as much light as possible to enter through three tall multi-coloured stained glass windows on one side of the room. A delicate hint of roses permeates the air.

In the space in between two of the windows sits a hand carved wooden desk with a fancy oval mirror centered precisely on the wall above it. The desk is flanked on both sides by two crystal lamps and an extremely ornate wicker chair. *I'm wrong, I'm still dreaming.* One entire wall of the room is a built-in bookshelf. When she looks at the words on the spines, they're made up of unrecognizable shapes and unfamiliar symbols. Amazed, she realizes she can translate the foreign language. Two books are called *The History of Yuetsion* and *The Atlas of Yuetsion*.

Quiet footsteps approach her door. Frozen in fear, she watches as the knob starts to turn. Phoebe lies down and shuts her eyes tightly, afraid of who, or what, might be on the other side of the door. A soft squeal of hinges indicates one of the doors has opened. She pretends to be asleep, holding her breath, as a strange bird's twitters fill the space.

"Quiet Riddy," a boy's voice says, as the footsteps get closer. She can even smell him, a faint non-human musk. "My goodness, she looks just like her."

Like who?

Curious, she opens her eyes and sits up. The boy jumps back, surprised. One look is enough to confirm he's not human. He appears to be the same age and height as her, but that's where the similarities end. His reptilian-like skin is blue and his chest and belly, where you can see them through his clothing, are a brilliant shade of violet, as are the palms of his hands and his lower jaw. Tufts of short navy blue hair can be seen sticking out from under his thin red toque, which features a pattern of yellow feathers that frame his face perfectly. He doesn't appear to have any eyebrows, unless his toque is just hiding them. His human-like eyes have green sclera and purple irises. His brown pants are designed with unique, swirly-lined aqua and green patterns and his open green vest, worn over a cream coloured muscle shirt, is comprised of whirly purplish designs. *What the heck am I looking at?! Unless I'm still dreaming, I don't know what's normal anymore!*

It suddenly hits Phoebe: the boy looks exactly like her dream twin, except he's a boy. On his shoulder sits one of the most striking birds she's ever seen. The tips of its tail feathers and wings begin in a shade of very light purple. As the colour gets closer to its body, it changes to a purple so dark it's almost black.

She points at the bird. "A bird!"

"Wh-what's a bird?"

What's a bird? WHAT'S A BIRD?! There's a bird standing right on your shoulder!

"Look, I'm sorry I scared you. I just wanted to check up on you," he says, cautiously stepping towards the bed. Mysty jumps off the bed to hide underneath it, sensing the tension of the moment. Phoebe keeps an eye on him as he inches closer. One of the symptoms of her autism is she can't handle close physical contact from someone she doesn't know or trust. This boy, or whatever he is, is invading her personal bubble.

"There's no reason for you to be afraid. I'm not going to hurt you," he says. He tentatively puts out a hand in order to greet her. "I'm-"

Phoebe cuts him off with a high-pitched shriek and hurries as quickly as she can to the wall with all of the bookshelves. The young boy, surprisingly agile on his lizard-like feet, chases her around the room as he continues his attempts to comfort her. Annoyed by all of the commotion, the purple bird on his shoulder lets out a loud squawk as it launches itself across the room. It lands on the desk in between the windows, ruffles its feathers and lets everyone in the room know exactly how upset it is.

"Please, I'm not going to hurt you!" the boy says.

Phoebe pitches a book at his head, and it smacks against his temple.

"Ow! Stop that!" He catches the next one with his right hand, then another with his left. "Would you please just settle down so that I can talk to you?"

By way of reply, Phoebe throws another book.

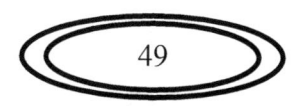

Swiftly, a scaly tail smacks the book from midair. It's blue, with a violet underbelly, and it swings club-like through the air.

HE HAS A TAIL?!!!

Phoebe had thought, or rather hoped, that these visions were imaginary. She still can't figure out if she's awake or asleep. She can't even tell if her kidnapping was a dream or not, since it felt as realistic as being in both the mirror halls and her current location.

Gently putting the books down on the ground, the lizard boy approaches Phoebe with hands outstretched in invitation. "Now-now, don't panic. I'm not going to harm you in any way." He pauses waiting to see what Phoebe's reaction will be.

"NO!"

Phoebe dashes frantically towards the double doors. In her agitated state she's not watching where she's going, so the sudden appearance of someone else in the room takes her completely by surprise. She bounces into someone's chest and crumples backwards to the floor.

"What on Yuetsion is going on here?!" the plump alien man says, looking down to where she's fallen in a heap. Looking up at the creature that had brought her to such an abrupt stop, Phoebe is once again rendered speechless. This older gentleman has many of the same reptilian characteristics as the boy. The yellow colouration of his bottom jaw, his large belly and palms contrasts the avocado green of the rest of his body. His head is hairless, with rough-looking scales, and the end of his long fat tail twitches on the floor. His calm gazing eyes are comprised of yellowish-green tinted sclera and aqua irises and he's wearing a black tunic with fiery abstract patterns that's not quite big enough to cover his whole gut. His orange-streaked pants feature a hole suitable for his tail, while straining grey suspenders pull taut from his shoulders.

"Oh! Yer awake. Here, let me help you up," he says, his voice a deep grumble. He bends to help her, but she backs away. "I'm sorry to have bumped into you. You came outta nowhere! I see you've already met Hezkale."

Phoebe stares back at the blue boy who smiles awkwardly, giving a timid wave of his hand. *Hez-kale?* "H-H-Hezkale?"

"That's correct. And I'm Yorgo," says the large man. "I know yer probably very frightened, but I assure you we're quite harmless." Yorgo tilts his head, concerned. "You must be starving. How about I make some breakfast for ya?"

Ignoring her stomach's stabbing hunger pangs, Phoebe continues to back away. She cannot afford to trust anyone in this strange world, no matter how friendly they may act. Turning her back, she rushes back to the safe haven of her bed, pausing only to grab Mysty from her hiding place. Cuddling the kitten protectively underneath one arm, Phoebe grasps a bedpost and stares suspiciously.

"Hmm...," Yorgo says, perplexed. "In that case you can just tell me when you want to eat somethin. We'll leave you alone for now."

Gesturing to Hezkale, he turns and starts heading out of the room. With a sigh of defeat, Hezkale slowly follows him. His bird Riddy, still squawking, soars off the desk and back onto Hezkale's shoulder.

"Very sorry I scared you," he says, closing the door gently behind him.

After watching the door for a couple of minutes to make sure no one else is going to make another unscheduled visit to her room, Phoebe leaves the safety of her bed and starts exploring. Drawn towards the windows, Phoebe ignores everything else. *Suppose I'm not dreaming. Am I in an unknown country? Am I even still in my world?* She pulls back the drapes and light cascades into the room, momentarily blinding her. She blinks her eyes until she can see a glass door leading out onto a stone carved balcony. Phoebe twists its bronze knob, swings the door wide open, and takes an exploratory step onto the balcony. Taking in a deep breath of fresh clean air, she's astounded by the beauty of the world around her. Elaborately carved stone towers and spires, topped with statues of mystical looking beings, seem to be touching the sky. Her towers' outside walls are shielded by outlandish statues. At the base of each tower, including her own, are the homes and shops of the inhabitants of this world. Looking down, Phoebe can see hundreds of the blue humanoids scurrying about.

In the far distance, she can just barely glimpse towering mountains that provide a ring of protection. Some appear to be forest-covered stone, while several of the other ones appear to be colossal crystals that look like gargantuan pieces of quartz. Phoebes thinks they resemble the minerals she's learned about in school—titanium quartz, bismuth, opal, fluorite, tourmaline, scolecite, realgar, uvarovite, crocoite, rhodochrosite, etc. by texture, brightly reflecting the sun's rays colourfully. Tropical forests can be seen on the outskirts of the city and a few trees covered in moss and smothered in vines stand in the midst of the city. Some look like giant palm trees with blue leaves and tall thin trunks. Others have a vast sphere of pink-orange leave. Another reminds her of the sequoia trees of California. Some of the trees are more than five-hundred metres high. Above her, cloud wisps drift across the sun. Farther up in the sky she can see one, two, three, four, five… seventeen moons up in the sky! They vary in colour and size, ranging from itsy moon to tiny planet-sized. Eight of them appear to have strangely similar features to Earth's moon, while the other nine have the appearance of gas planets. Seven of the gas moons are encircled by one to eight rings. She can practically make out every single specific colour the world has to offer, just by taking a random glimpse outside.

"Ace…"

A strange animal call, off to her left, startles Phoebe. She turns just in time to see a bat-like creature land on a nearby statue, gleaming yellow in the sun. Then it spreads its webbed wings and soars away at the sound of a loud, resounding gong. Phoebe plugs her ears, crouches to the ground, and cringes, counting. When she reaches nine, the clamour dies out. Does that mean it's 9:00? Does this world even operate on the same clock? She can't tell. It's this moment she realizes she must be standing on the town's clock. Feeling frightened and confused, she begins to hum her jam and heads back into the room for safety. This habitually calms her down after a panic attack, but unfortunately even this familiar tune isn't enough to calm her down this time.

What's going on?! Where am I?! What do they want from me?!...Where's my mother and father?! WHERE?! Sobbing hysterically, Phoebe reaches for the only familiar thing in the room: Mysty. Although she knows her parents aren't responsible, she's overwhelmed by a feeling of abandonment. She's completely alone in a foreign world where she doesn't know anyone.

Chapter 5

    The pealing tones of the clock tower inform Phoebe several hours have passed. Phoebe sits in the middle of the vast bed curled into a tight ball with Mysty tucked under her chin. The kitten's rumbling purr is a comfort to Phoebe. Except for her necklace, Mysty is the only other link to home. Phoebe's red-rimmed eyes and the smudged tear tracks on her cheeks are the only remaining evidence of the events from earlier in the day. She lays there in the quiet, mulling things over, until she finally decides the mirror chamber was a dream and the world she's currently in as reality, at least for the time being. It could be that both worlds are somehow intertwined, but she will reserve judgment until such time as she's able to fully comprehend what exactly is going on. She wishes she could control her nightmares in the same manner as her daydreams. It would sure help prove if recent events and her current situation are real or not. Maybe if she could figure out how to control her dreams, nightmares wouldn't even exist in her life.

Uncurling herself, she realizes she can't continue to isolate herself, a sentiment her grumbling stomach heartily seconds. *Maybe it's time for me to try to overcome my fears and make peace with these aliens. Maybe if I treat them nicely and explain how much my home means to me, they might return me back there.* As if the world is eavesdropping on her thoughts, a sharp rap on the door echoes through the room, followed shortly by an inquisitive face.

"Are you okay?" the woman asks. Even half-hidden by the door Phoebe can feel an aura of serenity surrounding her, and for a moment she forgets her fears.

The woman has similar colouring to Yorgo, and seems to belong to the same culture. She exudes femininity, with a slender frame and thick dark green eyebrows that have been smoothly plucked under her curly dark green hair, which is pulled back into a tidy ponytail. She's wearing a simple sheath-like dress in a hunter green which perfectly complements her hair. Red and black diamond patterns are interwoven into her dress, and the hem collects on the ground around her feet. She gazes at Phoebe with an astounded but gentle expression.

"My, my, you really do look like her!" the woman says.

"Huh?"

The woman smiles. "Allow me to introduce myself. My name is Hilmina. May I ask who you are?"

Hill-min-ah? Phoebe stares down at her hands, says nothing.

"Well, you don't have to tell me, if you don't want to. Can you understand what I'm saying at least?"

Phoebe nods her head. Hilmina looks at her incredulously.

"Amazing! Oh my, my!" she says. "This will definitely make things easier for me." Tilting her head to the side, she smiles reassuringly. "I understand you had a rather upsetting encounter with Hezkale and my husband Yorgo earlier today. Men can be so insensitive at times." She tilts her head and looks at Phoebe. "I bet you miss your family?"

Phoebe nods as tears once again start streaming down her cheeks.

"Oh, I'm so sorry! You poor child! Here, take this." Hilmina pulls out a red handkerchief from her pocket and Phoebe takes it, wiping away her tears and blowing her nose. When she offers it back, Hilmina grimaces good-naturedly. "You can keep it." Phoebe folds up the handkerchief and puts it in her skirt pocket, watching as Hilmina takes a place on the edge of her bed. "I'm very sorry that you were brought here against your will. Had I known you were just a child, I would've tried to prevent your kidnapping." She holds out her hand. "I may not be able to take you back home, but I can take you to a place I know of that might cheer you up."

Hilmina's gentle nature reminds Phoebe of her Aunt Matilda, her father's sister, who used to fly up from New Zealand to visit, making Hilmina seem more trustworthy than the previous two aliens. Struggling to maintain her composure, Phoebe takes a huge gulp of air. *If I'm ever going to stop crying, maybe I should try to stop thinking about my family for a bit. Now for Hilmina, should I trust her? I remember what stranger danger programs taught me about people seeming to be absolutely normal on the outside but rotten on the inside. But...I've already been stolen away by strangers into a completely different world so…I might just possibly be screwed no matter what decision I make now.*

Phoebe decides to take a huge risk and accept Hilmina's offer. Picking up Mysty, she reaches out and gingerly takes hold of Hilmina's hand.

"Great! You and your little friend can follow me."

Leading the way out of the bedroom, Hilmina begins to escort Phoebe through the different levels of the tower. As they make their way down long corridors and up and down a number of staircases, Phoebe tries to take in everything around her. The floors, walls and staircases are all decked out in colourful, well-detailed fractal patterns which seem to continue on endlessly. Bulky chandeliers covered in glitzy minerals hang daintily from the ceilings and elegantly cut crystals hang in richly decorated sconces on the walls. Dozens of framed paintings exhibit quixotic landscapes, alien creatures and portraits of the citizens of the planet. Each room they pass through has at least one statue.

The rooms are packed with many of the blue-hued residents, which Phoebe guesses must be the dominant race in this world. There are green ones too, wearing similar fashions, and red lizards that stand out more than the green ones. Unlike the green and blue ones, they have white skin from the lower jaws to the bottom ends of their tails, short sharp claws on both their fingers and toes and piercing pointy teeth. They have no hair whatsoever, eyes with blue irises surrounded by gold sclera and they give Phoebe the heebie jeebies. The red ones appear to be more formally dressed. The males are wearing dark long-sleeved tops with black slacks, while the females wear dresses of rich-looking fabric. They stare at Phoebe in disbelief as she passes, and she tries not to stare back. She attempts to focus on their tails, instead of their faces so that she doesn't feel so uncomfortable.

I'm surrounded by aliens! They're staring at me too! Stop that! You yourselves are more fascinating than me! Please take my mental advice if you all happen to have telepathic alien abilities! Oh man, I wonder what all of these strange things are even thinking about me. They're looking at me as if I'm a bomb with an unknown detonation time. Leading Phoebe outside, Hilmina pauses to give her a chance to adjust to the intense brightness. After blinking her eyes rapidly, Phoebe finally gets the chance to see where it is Hilmina has taken her. The beautiful vista spreading out before is bewildering—Hilmina has brought her to one of the most exquisitely designed gardens she's ever seen.

"I don't know very much about you, but what I do know is that I've never met a girl who doesn't like flowers. Feel free to explore here anytime you want. These gardens are open to everyone in the tower." Hilmina sits down on a conveniently placed bench to the right of the garden's entrance. "I'll be waiting here if you need me."

Ignoring the roughness of the gravel through her stocking feet, Phoebe slowly strides around the garden. Two large manicured bushes flank either side of the entrance to the garden. In one flower bed, oversized purple sunflowers, with tree-like stems, stretch to a height of thirty feet. Interspersed throughout the garden are numerous pieces of multi-hued stone minerals. Their disorganized placement appears to be a deliberate attempt at preventing the garden from becoming too formal. As she takes in all of this beauty, Phoebe can feel her stress lifting. Mysty, meanwhile, has had enough of being held and wants to explore the garden, too. Her attention has been captured by movement in the grass below. She wriggles until Phoebe places her on the ground then goes immediately into hunter mode. With her tail erect, she stalks tiny pink insects.

The sound of splashing water causes Phoebe to look around. To her left she discovers an attractive fountain made entirely of flamboyantly sculpted crystal. Mysty leaps onto the fountain's lowest rim and laps the shimmering water thirstily. Phoebe stretches out her hand and drags it through the fountain's trickling stream, which is refreshingly cool in the tropical heat. She unintentionally flicks some water onto Mysty, who meows in irritation. A loud humming sound draws Phoebe's attention away from the antics of her silly kitten. Focusing in the direction the vibrations are coming from, she's surprised to see an enormous red and blue hummingbird taking gentle sips of nectar from the enormous trumpet-shaped cup of a scarlet flower. The bird is literally as large as Phoebe is! She's buffeted by the breezes generated by its wings. It rapidly floats curiously up to her for a few seconds, startling her, only to fly by rocket-like.

"Cool!" *That's the biggest hummingbird I've ever seen!*

As the hummingbird flies off into the distance, Phoebe can hear the cheerful whistling of more birds nearby. She pauses to retrieve her feline before pushing her way through the foliage. She makes her way towards what turns out to be a rather substantial flock of alien birds. Some are a single colour, while others' feathers feature multi-coloured hues. Many are comparable in size to the house finches and chickadees she's used to, but there are some birds, like the hummingbird from a few moments earlier, which are extremely oversized. Others appear to be even tinier than the hummingbirds of Earth. One particular oddity is a miniature peacock, about the size of a rabbit, which struts across the grass showing off its beautiful tail. It emits an ear-piercing sound, making Phoebe recoil. Her jaw hangs slack—she has never seen so many birds in one place before. There's even more than in the Bloedel Conservatory in Vancouver!

"What a beautiful place." She looks down at Mysty. "I wonder if this is some type of bird sanctuary."

Mysty struggles in her hands. She doesn't care what this place is. All she wants to do is explore these unfamiliar surroundings. Phoebe sets her back down on the ground and the kitten quickly disappears underneath a nearby bush. Gazing around in admiration, Phoebe realizes the birds are mostly congregating around one particular tree. She can see it's some type of raspberry-like fruit tree with pink bark, which appears to be loaded with ripe fruit. Although Phoebe has watched birds eating fruit from the cherry trees in her backyard back home, it was nothing compared to the spectacle she's witnessing now. *This…this is a dream come true!*

Wanting to see the birds close up, she picks off one of the low-hanging berries and holds it out to her feathered friends. Eager to catch the attention of at least some of the birds, Phoebe lets loose with a whistle. Several birds break away and land on her outstretched hand. As they nibble chunks off the berry, she giggles as their small feet tickle her palm. A teeny green one, smaller than a hummingbird, has a squeaky whistle that's reminiscent of the hinges on the bedroom door her dad had recently oiled. It's like a fly with feathers.

"Beautiful!"

The sound of feet crunching across a gravel path prompts Phoebe to turn around. Hilmina, who had remained near the tower to give Phoebe some privacy, is now making her way down the path.

"My, my. It looks like you're enjoying yourself. I'm glad to see you're feeling better now."

A slight smile passes over Hilmina's features, but it quickly fades. Tears form in her eyes, and Phoebe doesn't know how to ask her what's wrong. She trails her finger down her cheek, signifying Hilmina's tears.

"Oh! It's nothing," Hilmina says. "Can you please excuse me?"

She moves away without looking back at Phoebe, while Phoebe stares at her curiously, forgetting about the birds and feeling sorry for the one person who has brought her joy in this world. *What was that all about? Did I do anything wrong? Why is she suddenly so sad?*

Chapter 6

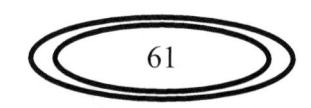

Fantastical garden creatures roam through Phoebe's mind as she gazes out at the extraordinary view below her balcony. The crisp, clean air conjures her childhood summer days, back in Vancouver, but it isn't the same. She runs her fingers over the intricately carved railings, leaning against them as she thinks about home. The sun begins its slow descent while dazzling displays of prismatic rainbows shimmer amidst the clouds and reflect off the crystalline mountains, their colours blindingly bright. Farther off she can see the dim outlines of multiple moons. It's almost as if they're waiting for their bigger and brighter cousin to stop showing off so they can reveal their unique night-time magic.

Mysty, who has been lazing on the railing of the balcony with one paw dangling as she watches the coming and goings of the aliens below, meows happily. She pads over for attention, receives a tender scratch behind the ear and responds with a contented, rumbling purr. She leaps from the railing and traipses back into the extravagance of Phoebe's new bedroom with her tail proudly upright. Phoebe follows closely behind, leaving the sky's magnificence for another time. Immediately she's met with the sight of the extremely disorganized bookshelf on one side, which makes her feel uncomfortable—like many autistics, she can't stand when things are out of place.

If those aliens would kidnap me against my will and make up for it by providing me with a room that screams royalty, the least they could do is make it more presentable. Creating a plan of attack to conquer this chaos, she decides to arrange the books according to the colours of their protective dust jackets. She carefully places books back on the shelves, staring at their strange lettering. Her sudden ability to understand this foreign language, although helpful, has left her very confused. She cannot understand how or why she has suddenly become a linguistics expert.

"I wonder why I can understand this language," she says.

Mysty meows in response.

Once she's placed the last book, Phoebe takes a step backwards to inspect her work. Once again she's defeated the enemy known as clutter.

A sudden rap of knuckles against her bedroom doors interrupts her reverie, and she scrambles back a couple steps and peers at the door anxiously. Without bothering to wait for her permission, Hilmina and Yorgo swing open the door and march inside.

"Hello," Yorgo says, cheerfully. "Sorry to disturb you, but Cernin would like ta see you."

Sir-nin? Who's that?

"Don't worry, he's really friendly," Hilmina says. "We'll take you to him."

Well, at least Hilmina will be by my side. Perhaps I'll finally be able to get some straight answers about why I'm here, and whether or not this is all a dream. Phoebe picks up Mysty and clutches her close, then tentatively approaches the pair. Yorgo leans in for a closer look, looming.

"Say, who's this cute lil fella?" he asks, reaching out to pet her. Mysty hisses and swipes, making him jump back. "Sheesh! Though not very friendly."

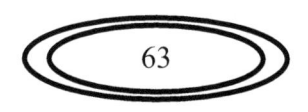

Phoebe can't help but smile, hiding a chuckle, as Mysty continues to meow aggressively. Even Hilmina shields her mouth to hide a laugh. *Sorry, Mysty is highly aggressive towards strangers.*

"Alright then, follow us," Yorgo says, waving them along.

Yorgo leads them down a series of passageways. The décor flashes by too quickly for her to identify anything, and she strains to keep up with his quick-paced stride. Hilmina follows closely behind, her hunter green dress rustling loudly. They appear to be heading in the opposite direction of her previous excursion through the confusing corridors. Lizard people, mainly blue in colour, gape at Phoebe as she steps past them, making her feel very awkward. She can hear faint whispers of conversation as they pass. The continuous swaying of Yorgo's long tail acts like a hypnotist's watch, drawing her into a trance-like state.

"It's considered rude to stare at someone's tail," Hilmina whispers, momentarily distracting her. But even with this warning, her eyes still gravitate towards the pointed, dinosaur-like appendage, making Hilmina sigh. The three of them arrive at a set of large double doors edged in pure gold decked with diamond shaped crystals the size of Phoebe's head. With an annoyed grunt, Yorgo pushes them open.

Phoebe gapes in wonder. Shaped like a vertical cylinder, the ceiling is over a hundred feet above their heads. Spiral staircases lead the way up to numerous floors and all around them are enormous stained glass windows, their curtains drawn back to provide as much natural light as possible. It appears to be a huge laboratory. Tidy lines of test tubes rest in holders, covering nearly every available surface. The liquids inside them are dazzlingly vivid, bright, and many of them seem to glow with a soft, ethereal light. Behind these counters red, green and blue lizard-like beings, many of whom are wearing protective goggles and black lab coats, work with the chemicals—mixing them, pouring them, examining them. Test tubes steam. In one corner, she can see two aliens, one blue and one red, who appear to be in a very heated discussion.

As the trio slowly make their way through the room, the vapour coming out of the test tubes fogs up Phoebe's glasses. She wipes her glasses on the hem of her shirt and pushes them back into place. Glancing around, she spots Hezkale. His purple bird is nearby, bathing itself in a small dish of water. He gives her a wave, but she glances away shyly.

"Cernin! We've brought her!" Yorgo yells.

"Look out below!" a man's voice shouts from up above. Phoebe watches as a rather red lizard being slides down one of the stair banisters, holding a vial of crimson fluid in his right hand. Crash-landing on the floor, he trips and smashes into a long table crowded with glowing test tubes. The chemicals within them begin to steam, jostled, but squinting through her once-again fogged lenses, Phoebe realizes none of the beings in the room are overly concerned. He gets up and steps through the cloud, holding up the liquid triumphantly in one hand. He hoists it toward the ceiling. "Aha! It's still alive!"

Phoebe once again wipes her glasses on the hem of her shirt and then replaces them. Through her freshly cleaned lenses, she gets her first real look at this new creature. He's skinny, with white skin on his bottom jaw, palms and the bottom side of his tail, the rest of him a fiery colour like blood. His golden eyes feature sky blue irises. His lab coat is speckled with chemical spots, he wears a monocle on his left eye and the claws of his feet click against the floor, jutting out from his tattered-looking black shoes. He grins, exposing a shark-like row of chompers, which makes Phoebe feel extremely nervous. She hugs Mysty to her chest. *He'd better not eat people with teeth like that!* Mysty meows in irritation, letting Phoebe know she's squeezing her too firmly.

"I saved the formula from spilling," he says in a higher-pitched, more formal voice than Yorgo's.

"My, my Cernin. Would it hurt to just walk down the stairs for once?" Hilmina asks in annoyance.

"Probably, but it wouldn't be as grand an entrance." Cernin looks over at Phoebe and winks.

So this is Cernin. He's dressed like a scientist and seems to work with these fluids, so he must be a scientist. Maybe he's smart enough to give me all the answers I need.

As the other creatures tidy up Cernin's mess, he strides quickly to another table. He mixes the chemical in his vial with a green one and the resulting chemical reaction creates a mixture that's such a deep shade of blue it's almost purple. Cernin sniffs it, sighs happily and holds it up to Phoebe.

"Drink up," he says.

Phoebe stares down uneasily at the brew, wrinkling her nose with distaste. Drinking unknown liquids is not high on her list of favourite things to do.

"Don't worry, it's quite safe."

Phoebe places Mysty on the ground next to her. She takes the test tube and sips slowly. The taste is so vile she flinches, accidentally spilling a bit of on the floor. She immediately spits it out, places the drink on a nearby table and turns towards Cernin with disgust.

"Awful!"

"But healthy," Cernin says.

Mysty observes the puddle on the floor and sniffs it. She licks it and shakes her head, hissing in disgust.

Cernin adjusts his monocle. "So you're indeed one of the uishanoles we've been looking for."

You-ee-shan-ole?

"The resemblance is definitely amazing now that I can see you in the proper light. Oh!" Cernin startles Phoebe. "Your eyes are mismatched! How infrequently extroadinrary! What's your name?"

Phoebe frowns, shaking her head. These aliens are perfect strangers to her and she was taught from an early age to never reveal her name to strangers. Never.

"Hmm…I understand…You don't know us or trust us enough yet to reveal your name to us." He taps his finger on his chin as he walks slowly around Phoebe. "How about we call you…Qelphy instead? Is that alright with you?"

Kell-fee…Hmm…It does sound rather cute. I kind of like it. Phoebe nods relieved they're not going to force the issue.

"Qelphy it is! Now, Qelphy, I was told that you can speak Brimcolf," Cernin says. His voice is loaded with curiosity.

"Ex…cuse me?" Phoebe says.

"Brimcolf. It's our native language and yet you, an outsider, can understand it perfectly. But the question is how?"

That's what I've been asking myself. Hmm…I think I started understanding Brimcolf ever since I was in that mirror labyrinth…

"Hmm…" Cernin says. "Perhaps your planet's language has enough similarities to Brimcolf that it makes it easy for you to decipher it. By the way, what's your native language?"

"Eng…English." The stammer in her voice portrays her nervousness.

"English…Fascinating…Very fascinating…What's your planet called?"

"Earth…"

"Okay, your nationality?"

"Canadian."

"Can-a-di-an. That's got a nice ring. Could you stick out your tongue?"

Confused, she sticks out her tongue. *I need my questions answered more than yours!*

"Hmm...Interesting...your insides are pinkish-reddish, instead of violet," Cernin says.

"V-Violet?"

"Yes! All of the creatures' insides in your world are most likely red, while all of the insides of the creatures in this world are violet. See?" Cernin sticks his tongue out, showing off its violet colour, astounding and weirding Phoebe out simultaneously. "Please forgive me. I just love making new discoveries."

He chuckles excitedly.

Phoebe sighs in annoyance. *I really can't take you seriously Cernin. Looks like the only way I'm going to get my questions answered is if I speak them out.*

"I want-"

"Oh!" Cernin snaps. "Hold that thought." He quickly jogs over to a table, picking up a test tube filled with an oily black substance. As he sniffs it, his whole body, including his tail, shivers in disgust and he smiles. "Perfect!" He puts a cork in the test tube. "You up there! Catch!" Cernin calls up to a blue lizard woman. He tosses the chemical up two floors and she catches it.

"That was dangerous Cernin!" Hilmina says. The annoyance in her voice can be felt by everyone in the room.

"Don't worry, it's safe-"

"I-I want explanations right now," Phoebe demands, forcing out her words.

"Perfect! That's exactly why I asked for you to come here: to explain everything to you." He walks over to a shelf and picks up an object which looks like a silver scepter with a red crystal orb at the end of it. "I prefer to explain things visually, if you don't mind."

Phoebe nods, focusing intently on the scepter, knowing they can perform very amazing abilities in this alien world. *I learn better visually anyways.* "So, wh-where am I?"

The scepter's red crystal begins to glow. The room around them seems to disappear and, as if by magic, an illusion of outer space surrounds them. *What's all this?!* She can see nebulas, stars, comets, meteors, stardust and planets all around her. It's as if she and the other beings are literally floating around in outer space. Mysty steps about on the ground uneasily and pats her paws against it repeatedly, confused. The purple bird hops out from the wet dish and shakes its feathers dry before ascending to Hezkale's shoulder. A large planet with unfamiliar continents and oceans forms right in front of them. Phoebe counts thirty-four moons of varying colours, shapes and sizes surrounding it. Based on the magical diagram, seventeen moons are floating in the daytime area and seventeen float about on the night side of the planet. Seventeen of them are made up of various gases and fourteen of them are encircled by one to ten rings, while the remaining moons are made of stone.

"Ace," Phoebe says.

Cernin points his staff towards the planet. "You're currently here, on Yuetsion. It's located within the Jaeliff galaxy of our universe." A section of one of the continents glows. "Right now we're in the city of Rundrick, in the country Veshael. More specifically, we're inside the laboratory located in the Hiljin Tower. Its purpose is to gather information."

"Amazing...But how did I get here?"

"That's easy. We used magic," Cernin explains.

"Magic?! But...that's impossible! Magic doesn't ex-exist, at least...not in the way that I think you're talking about. It's-It's all about making the audience believe something is happening through the use of illusion and other tricks."

"Perhaps it doesn't exist in your world or even your universe, but there's plenty of it here," Cernin says holding the scepter closer to Phoebe, giving her a closer look. "See this? This is my scepter. It casts a number of different spells, which you'll soon be taught. We used my scepter's magic to create a spell allowing us to open a portal so we could travel through dimensions."

"Dimension travelling?!"

"Not only are you on a different planet, but you're also now in a completely different universe," Cernin explains, raising his arms for emphasis. "I'll explain how the magic of this world works as soon as I tell you why you're here."

"If this di-dimension has nothing to do with my dimension then...are you aliens?"

"Aliens?" Hezkale asks. He had quietly been making his way towards Cernin and the others and had only caught the last portion of the conversation.

"We're not aliens, we're yuets," Cernin says.

"Yuets?"

"Yes, we're yuets. All of the beings living on this planet are called yuets. I'm a yuet. Hezkale, Hilmina and Yorgo are yuets. We're all yuets, except you, of course, Qelphy. Are you an alien, if that's what you call it?"

"Well, since I-I am not from this world…I guess I would say so."

"Aha! So all of your kind are called aliens," Cernin says excitedly.

"No. We-we're humans or-or people,"

"But you just told me you were an alien."

"Yes, but we're not aliens on my planet."

"So…you're an alien here, but not where you're from," Cernin says, trying to understand. Phoebe sighs in frustration.

"Where I come from, alien means foreign."

"Ahh…I see," Cernin says. "So we yuets must be aliens to you and your kind then."

Phoebe nods. "Definitely."

"Okay, so what are you really called then?"

"A person, a human, a human being."

"So that's what you're called. Would it be persons and humans for multiples?" Cernin asks.

"Yes, or people."

Hezkale breaks into the conversation. "Your…'people' are very fascinating."

"Yes, I must admit that Cernin, Hezkale and I found yer world pretty interesting. But we had to go out of our way to make sure that none of your…'humans' spotted us," Yorgo says with a chuckle.

A sudden realization hits Phoebe. She recognizes Cernin, Hezkale and Yorgo from that stormy night, especially their voices! The shapes of their bodies and the details of their eyes are firmly imprinted in her brain. "You're the kidnappers!" Phoebe shouts. The image of Yuetsion dissolves and everybody stops to stare.

Cernin sighs. "Yes, Qelphy. We did kidnap you, but we can explain why." Phoebe backs away a bit for protection. "Now, don't be afraid. We have no intention of hurting you."

"But…why kidnap me?" Phoebe asks.

Leaning forward, Cernin looks at her with a serious expression on his face. "Because you may be Yuetsion's last hope."

"Last…hope?"

"Yes, you see. You are the uishanole of Princess Vehilia."

Veh-hill-ee-a?

"What-what is a…uishanole and who's Princess…Vehilia?!" She's becoming increasingly frustrated with all she is being expected to take in.

"This is Princess Vehilia." Cernin uses his scepter to create an illusion of Princess Vehilia. Speechless, Phoebe stares at the image in amazement as it comes into focus. It's the same blue girl from her dreams. Except for the difference in body colour and the fact she's reptilian, Vehilia could pass for Phoebe's twin. Cernin places an image of Phoebe right beside Vehilia's image and it's uncanny how alike—and yet how different—the two girls are.

"You see, uishanole means 'impersonator' or 'copy'. A simpler meaning for uishanole is: a reflection of someone from a different world or dimension. And as you can see, there's no doubt you are Princess Vehilia's uishanole, her reflection."

Eyes wide, Phoebe gazes at Vehilia's image. *A reflection…I think my dream is starting to make a little more sense now. The Princess Vehilia in my dream was trying to show me I am more than who I think I am. Amazing! I am a reflection of a princess from a different world! A world of magic! A fantasy world, like I've always dreamed of visiting! What an ace! But, how does that scary, shadowy monster that tried to eat me in my dream factor into all of this? Should I consider that to be a message too? And not only that, but how did I even dream about all that before all of this information? Maybe…this is all just coincidental. It must be.*

With all of this new information, Phoebe senses the oncoming twinges of a headache. One of the symptoms of her autism is her brain has never been good at handling or processing information overload. Phoebe begins to wonder what exactly it is these yuets expect her to do. She's broken out of her contemplations by Cernin's voice.

"Perhaps, since you're Vehilia's uishanole, you might just be able to wield the Vinston Scepter."

"Vinston Scepter?"

Cernin nods his head. "It's considered by all, to be one of the most powerful scepters of Yuetsion!"

"You want-want me to wield a powerful scepter?! You want me to be your rescuer?! But-but why me and…s-s-save you from what?! And why me particularly?!"

"It's a long story, Qelphy, so please pay close attention."

Phoebe nods her head still trying to make sense of it all.

"To make things as sensible as I can for you, I will start by telling you the history of Yuetsion. You'll need to know about it anyways in order for you to fully understand your position in this world." Normally Phoebe dozes off during her teacher's history lectures due to extreme boredom, but she's so desperate to find out everything she must know. Cernin creates a magical image of the lands of Yuetsion and clears his throat.

"Millions of years ago, the yuets of this planet lived in a world that did not know the meaning of pure evil. We were a happy race seeking to live in peace and harmony with our fellow yuets. That is, until one particular yuet came along."

With a wave of his hand, Cernin creates a shadowy image of a yuet man that looks like Cernin's kind. However, even in this faded representation, Phoebe can see the evil glint in his eye. "He too was a yuet, just like all of us. More specifically, a Kume. This yuet hated all of the other inhabitants of Yuetsion. He considered everyone and every other creature to be useless and completely beneath his contempt. His hatred for yuets was so strong he could not even bear to look upon his own reflection."

Cernin pauses. The seriousness of his expression proves this is not some fairy tale he's telling her, but a true piece of Yuetsion's history.

"This yuet was so consumed with changing himself into something other than what he was that he isolated himself in a cave located in the farthest explored regions of our continent. His overall intentions were to become an immortal being with endless power, capable of subjugating all who got in his way. In other words, he wanted to be worshipped like a king of all monarchs." The images in the hologram change and Phoebe can see an inky darkness overpowering one small corner of the continent. "Hiding out in this cave he was free to practice his spells of dark magic that were so dangerous and permanent in use they had long been forbidden by our yuets. Surprisingly, even though his spells grew increasingly more powerful, he never attempted to use them on the other yuets he so despised. Instead, he consumed the spells like food and contained every bit of them inside of himself. He used the power of the spells to make himself stronger. As he continued to consume endless numbers of increasingly stronger spells, the dark magic began to change everything about him that had once been a yuet. It soon settled into his mind and spirit, leaving nothing behind of his true yuet self, turning him into something far worse than his original state mentally…and physically."

Cernin makes an image appear of a malicious yuet changing slowly into a terrifying monster, darkening the whole room further and further as it changes. The image grows darker as the transformation continues. Phoebe, along with everyone else in the room, observes the image frozen in fear. Mysty backs up against Phoebe's legs, shivering, so she picks her up and strokes her back. The bird on Hezkale's shoulder climbs down his shirt and wriggles into his pant pocket, hiding itself.

"With each new transformation, more of what had made him a yuet faded away, but the changes to his body were even more drastic," Cernin says. The yuet's skin changes from white to brown on his belly, chest, neck's front, palms and lower section of his ginormous tail and red to pitch black throughout the rest of his body and seems to ooze a trail of dark magic with every step he takes. His blackened claws and blade-like teeth dramatically increase. He grows two giant spiky webbed wings and a gargantuan third eye appears in the middle of his chest, unblinking and evil-looking.

What the heck am I looking at?!

"As this creature continued to devour more and more dark magic," Cernin goes on, "he became the colossal monster he had always wanted to be. Always hungry for more power, he eventually turned his attention towards the rest of the world. He overthrew the reigning monarchs of the time and set himself up as the supreme ruler. The evilness of his reign spread throughout the lands, like a blanket of thick black fog. It blotted out all of the light he so detested."

Pausing for dramatic effect, Cernin removes his monocle and wipes it quickly with the sleeve of his lab coat. "The terror of his reign was so ingrained in the hearts of the yuets and in their descendants that even today the sound of his name is enough to make yuets shake in fear. His name is…Gaphanagon."

A giant winged monster, surrounded by many other vicious-looking creatures, appears. As the group of evil monsters make their way across the lands of Yuetsion, a trail of chaos and destruction is left behind. Although the image is but a shadowy representation, it's realistic enough that all work in the room grinds fearfully to a halt.

Phoebe wishes she could get a better look at Gaphanagon, but she can only make out a few rudimentary details. Based on the magic holographic background, he appears to be about five-hundred metres tall!

Cernin proceeds with his narrative. "All of the magic Gaphanagon had consumed soon made him unstoppable. Through the use of only his hands, he was able to cast spells of immense powers. His endless supply of magic allowed him to create servants and spies that would help him to succeed in overtaking all of Yuetsion. These creatures wreaked havoc wherever they went. But worst of all, Gaphanagon had developed an appetite for fresh meat. His favourite snack was eating…yuets."

Phoebe gapes at Cernin in boundless shock. "He was…can-cannibalistic too?"

"Very. He could gobble up hundreds of his subjects at one single meal." Focusing back on the image, Cernin drew everyone's attention to the single eye in the middle of Gaphanagon's chest. "Not only was he cannibalistic, but the giant eye in the middle of his chest enabled him to suck yuets into it, thereby entrapping any yuets within who didn't do his bidding. To this day, no one knows what happened to them. Some yuets say this was just a more gruesome way to be eaten and yet there are others who insist there was a frightening world filled with horrific creatures and pain inside."

"You mean to tell me that-that creature actually existed?" Phoebe feels her fears escalating fast. All she wants to do is go back to the sanctuary of her room in her world. Mysty shuts her eyes and pushes her head against Phoebe's chest, in an attempt to ignore the disturbing vision.

"Yes. I'm afraid so."

Squinting as she inspects the illusion, Phoebe turns to Cernin and asks, "Why is the image so blurry?"

"I made the image blurry because it makes Gaphanagon less terrifying to look at. None of us can handle looking at his true image. His features are far too fearsome for even the bravest of yuets to take in, but most of all…his eyes."

"His eyes?" Phoebe asks, looking at Gaphanagon's three eyes, only displayed as blank white spaces.

"Yes, his eyes," Cernin says. "All yuets have gone out of our way for millions of years to completely forget about what his eyes looked like, they were that frightening. No one has a clue as to what his eyes look like nowadays…and for good reason too. Even a blurred image of Gaphanagon can have a negative impact on the unprepared…"

Oh, now you tell me.

As Gaphanagon's image slowly disappears the room brightens up and everyone in the room breathes a huge sigh of relief. The bird flies out of Hezkale's pocket, perching back on his shoulder. Mysty stops pressing her face against Phoebe.

"But…what did that monster have to do with the Vinston Scepter?" Phoebe asks.

"I'm getting there now, Qelphy," Cernin says. "So, at this point in our history, I'm sad to say no one on our planet possessed the powers needed to stop the evilness of Gaphanagon's reign." Cernin's scepter projects an image of two more impressive-looking scepters. "That is until the day that the two most powerful races of the yuets, the Veshaels and the Xeffizens, discovered two extraordinary crystals and used them to create a pair of extremely powerful scepters: the Vinston Scepter and Monston Scepter." The first scepter, if placed next to Hezkale, would be roughly his height. Its ebony shaft is as smooth as glass. Mounted at its top is a statuette of a monstrous lizard-like head, complete with razor sharp fangs and fierce, glowing green crystal eyes. It clenches a green crystal tightly in its' mouth.

As Phoebe gazes at the second of the two scepters, she's acutely aware that it appears to be a virtual replica of the one which had played such a prominent role in her dream. Inspecting it more closely, she concludes that it *is* the exact same scepter. The smooth surfaces of the ebony coloured shaft and the blue crystal imbedded in its top are exactly as she remembered. Even the black bird, poised as if waiting for an opportunity to take flight, is too realistic to be anything other than the real thing. The only similarity between the Vinston Scepter and Monston Scepter is their crystal sphere size.

Na-uh, this has to be coincidental just like Princess Vehilia!

The image of the larger scepter disappears, making the blue crystal scepter more prominent. "This is the Vinston Scepter. The creature sitting on top of it, that you have been calling a bird from what Hezkale told me, is in our tongue known as a mincy. Some of the strongest magic casters of that time cast a powerful spell on the scepter which would make it impossible for anyone not of the Veshael royal bloodline to be able to wield it, as a way of making sure no evil could ever use it. Not even Gaphanagon."

Cernin recreates the Monston Scepter at the forefront. "The Monston Scepter was created to work in the exact same way as the Vinston Scepter. However, the spell cast on it was designed to prevent anyone not of the Xeffizen royal bloodline from using it. The creature sitting on top of it, known as a kilquis, is a symbol which has long been used on the crests of the protectors of the Xeffizen royal family."

Cernin pauses and beckons one of the others in the lab to hand him a glass of water. He takes a sip and spits it out with disgust. "Bah! Tepid water."

Setting the rejected glass of water down on a nearby table, Cernin continues on with his explanation. "Both scepters contained enough magic to make it impossible for any of Gaphanagon's supporters to be able to get anywhere near them." The holographic images blur and sharpen up again, presenting Phoebe with what appears to be a colossal battle taking place. "The Veshaels and Xeffizens realize they could only beat Gaphanagon by uniting together the magical powers residing in each scepter, which they successfully did. This war between Gaphanagon and the two scepters was the Galprem War. After defeating Gaphanagon and winning the Galprem War, the yuets sealed and buried his body away in an underground cavern somewhere inside the Dontreden Lands. Once again, the yuets could enjoy a life of peace and prosperity, as the darkness created by Gaphanagon's reign slowly faded away."

"If Gaphanagon has been defeated, why do you need me?" Phoebe turns back to Cernin in confusion. At the same time, Mysty pats her paws against Phoebe, persuading her to scratch an itchy spot on her head.

"Let me explain," Cernin says. "Several generations after the defeat of Gaphanagon, the Xeffizens, seemingly out of nowhere, began changing from a society that promoted peace into one intent on the merciless destruction of those around them. Former allies became enemies and any alliances which had been made were being broken at an alarming rate. This drastic transformation is believed to have begun at the start of King Mistulboe's reign and no one has a concrete explanation for why it happened. All we know is we were faced with a new enemy with an extremely powerful weapon in their hands."

"The Monston Scepter?" Phoebe asks.

"That's correct, Qelphy."

Phoebe beholds a number of blue coloured yuets standing side by side in a perfect line, including Princess Vehilia. She assumes these are members of the Veshael royal family. "The Veshaels were determined to put a stop to the threat the Xeffizens posed and the only way this could be achieved was for the royal family to use the Vinston Scepter as a weapon once again against the Xeffizens. This war between the Veshaels and the Xeffizens was the Kendent War."

Cernin shakes his head as he looks gloomily at the images of the Veshaels.

"Unfortunately, the Xeffizens were clever enough, and more powerful. Every member of the royal bloodline was wiped out except for one: Princess Vehilia. She was the last one capable of controlling the power residing in the Vinston Scepter."

"S-so Princess Vehilia was p-princess of the Veshaels, the blue yuets?"

"Yes indeed Qelphy. Veshaels are native to this country and just like Hezkale over there; they all sport the same vibrant shade of blue." Hezkale nods his head as Cernin points in his direction.

"Well, are you a Xeff...Xeff...," Phoebe struggles as she tries to pronounce Xeffizen.

"A Xeffizen?" Cernin asks. "Oh no, I'm a Kume. We're easily identifiable by our red skin. Not that I would mean to brag, but I'm considered to be quite a handsome specimen, just ask my wife."

Hezkale snorts at this. Cernin glares at him.

"So...you're a Kume just like...Gaph-an-a-gon?" Phoebe asks.

"...Yes...Sadly yes...," His skin takes on a somewhat greyish cast. "Gaphanagon was a very horrible example of a Kume. We try not to dwell on that very dark part of our history."

"Well...what about them?" Phoebe asks pointing at Hilmina and Yorgo.

"We're Herynes. We're the green yuets of this world." Yorgo explains, wrapping his arm around Hilmina's shoulder.

"Then...what do the Xeffizens look like?" Phoebe asks.

Cernin pauses momentarily, uncertain of how to respond. He peers anxiously over at Hezkale, Hilmina and Yorgo. Hezkale waves his hand, signaling Cernin to carry on.

"Well…um…They look like…Kumes pretty much, only…they have different coloured skin and they're…a little bigger." Although confused by Cernin's refusal to deliver a proper description of the Xeffizens, Phoebe feels it's not really important at this time.

"Are all Xeffizens bad?"

"They sure are," Hezkale says. The mincy on his shoulder chirps in a deeper tone bobbing its head up and down, agreeing with the statement.

"Yes, I'm afraid Hezkale's right. It's extremely rare to come across one that isn't." He scratches his head. "Now where was I?"

"You were talking about Princess Vehilia being the last of the Veshaelian royal bloodline," Hilmina reminds Cernin.

"Ah! Yes!" Cernin snaps his fingers. "Thank you! As the sole remaining member of the royal family, Princess Vehilia inherited a very sad legacy. It was now her responsibility to protect the Veshaels from attack. Luckily, she somehow strategized clever enough fighting and spell casting tactics to allow her to defeat King Mistulboe. But sadly, just like the rest of her family, Vehilia's life was cut short when Mistulboe's son, Prince Zexen attacked her, stabbing her in the back. Her death ended the Kendent War. But the threat is still out there as long as Zexen, who's the current ruler of the Xeffizens, remains on the throne."

The crystal on Cernin's scepter dims and all of the projected illusions disappear. As the images fade away, Phoebe overhears Hezkale trying to choke back a sob. Looking over at him, she sees his tail sagging miserably and a painful expression flashing across his face before he drops his gaze down to his feet. His mincy rubs its head and wing against his neck in an attempt to cheer him up, but it doesn't do much at all.

Poor Hezkale, being a Veshael, he must have had it very hard. Cernin's history lesson must have been very difficult for him to get through.

"Although the Veshaels were able to defeat King Mistulboe, many of them had already been taken hostage and were forced into slavery. Most of their allies also suffered similar fates." Cernin reaches for a book entitled *The Veshael Royal Family* on the table behind him. "Given the terrible losses that had been suffered and the fact there were now no surviving members of the royal bloodline, it was feared no one would ever be able to wield the Vinston Scepter again."

Cernin pages through several chapters of the book before finally settling on the page he's been looking for and lifts his head towards Phoebe with a smile. "It was while I was doing research on Vehilia's family history I came across several obscure references to 'reflections' and something the author kept referring to as 'uishanoles'. Something about that term made me want to dig deeper. After going through the whole book without any results, it occurred to me that maybe I was looking in the wrong place. So I went to another possible place for answers."

Slamming the book, Cernin grabs another book titled *Mythologies of Yuetsion* and points at Hezkale. Phoebe watches in astonishment as Hezkale's pained expression from mere moments earlier changes into a toothy grin. The cheeky teenager bounces up and down in anticipation with his mincy wobbling, trying to keep balance. "I found my answers in the schoolbooks of a young lad who had a penchant for insubordination." Hezkale responds to this accusation by sticking out his tongue and crossing his eyes. "I would've known about this book sooner if it weren't so private."

"All along," Cernin continues, "the answers had been right in front of me. After paging through Hezkale's mythology book, I finally found what I was looking for. You see, Qelphy, the legends of uishanoles have become so obscure over the years that only the royal family still believed in their existence. To the rest of the population, they had become nothing more than stories we would tell our children."

Cernin shows Phoebe the page from Hezkale's schoolbook, providing the evidence he had been seeking. "As the revelation of the existence of uishanoles began to sink in, I was also left wondering how many other secrets the royal family had been keeping from us. So I went back to my original research and buried in an obscure passage, I found the instructions for a spell which had the ability to allow yuets to cross into other dimensions."

Cernin picks up a single document from the table and Phoebe catches a glimpse of diagrams and complex mathematical equations. "At some point in the past, yuets had used this spell to discover new worlds and it was while they were travelling to these new worlds that a few of them discovered the existence of uishanoles. Unfortunately, no one was ever able to bring back any physical evidence, so the stories of uishanoles began to fade into legend." Cernin folds the page and lays it back on the table. "It should also be noted that many of the yuets who crossed into other worlds were unable to return to Yuetsion. The dangers associated with dimension travelling became such a concern, that the royal families issued an edict officially banning its use."

As Cernin pauses for a breath, Phoebe blurts out, "But how were you able to find me if the use of dimension travel was banned?"

Cernin shifts awkwardly as he glimpses across at Hezkale and Yorgo. "Sometimes the only thing you can do is break the rules. But look at it this way, if we hadn't broken the rules, we wouldn't have proof uishanoles truly exist after all. You, Qelphy, are the very first uishanole to enter into the world of Yuetsion!"

I guess if Cernin and the others can be rule breakers, than it only makes sense that I can be a record breaker. Phoebe feels somehow honoured at the idea of being the first human to enter Yuetsion, but she still can't help feeling angry at the way she had been brought into this world in the first place.

"Armed with all of this new information, I devised a plan to retrieve the nearest Veshaelian uishanole. It was my belief there was someone out there with enough of a resemblance to any of the royal-blooded Veshaels they could trick the Vinston Scepter into accepting them as one of the royal family."

Cernin gestures his hand to the lab behind him. "Using my own funds, I created a private group which would be able to help me with this extremely dangerous and slightly illegal scheme. Using the combined efforts of multiple yuets, we were able to do the impossible. You stand before us today as proof of the successes of our endeavours."

"But-but how-how did you find me?"

"That question has an exceptionally easy answer. I used the spell Pundlaboa to allow us to travel to the dimension you reside in and to find you within your world."

"Pundla…what?" Phoebe tries to wrap her tongue around the unfamiliar word with Mysty cocking her head, meowing in a questioning tone.

"Pundlaboa, it's a secret spell only Veshaels know about. It's a very strong spell that once invoked, has the power to show the way to whatever you most desire. This is how it works." Cernin clears his throat and holds up his scepter. "Pundlaboa, I desire the…royal blooded Veshaelian…uishanole."

Cernin's scepter pulsates with an orange light slowly forming into a shimmering stream, which aims directly towards Phoebe. Phoebe's eyes widen, recognizing the spell. *That's the same spell Cernin cast into that magical underground vortex, which must've been the dimension spell.* The spell practically works in the same way as a compass guiding someone towards their destination, except much simpler.

"It's also very helpful for finding lost objects." Sighing, Cernin extinguishes the light from the crystal, which quickly winks out. "Bringing you here was an exceedingly great risk. There were a lot of things that could've gone wrong. But I firmly believe it was really worth the effort. Being that you're most definitely Vehilia's uishanole, we'll hopefully be able to get the Vinston Scepter to work for you and use it to destroy the Monston Scepter to make the Xeffizens surrender permanently." He holds out his scepter to Phoebe. "Until we're able to retrieve it, you may use my scepter. Any questions?"

The long historical narrative coupled with the revelation she's, quite possibly, the rescuer of an entire world leaves Phoebe with a headache. The more she thinks about the huge responsibility she has been given, the more anxious she becomes. She has never been one to take risks and yet here she's being asked to defend strangers from an entire race of dangerous lizard-like beings. Sweat drips down her back and her breathing speeds up. She's close to hyperventilation. Gripping her necklace tightly, she struggles to fight off the panic attack she knows is coming. As best as she can, working her brain in the hardest way ever, she tries to figure out ideas to persuade them to return her home.

"But…aren't there other uishanoles in my w-world you could use instead?"

Cernin shakes his head. "You actually are the only uishanole available in your world."

Phoebe stares at him in fear. "What?! How?!"

Mysty meows, pushing against Phoebe, wanting to be let down and Phoebe lightly places her to the ground. She rubs herself against Phoebe's legs, trying to help chill her out.

"You see, when the spell Pundlaboa led us to you, we didn't like the idea of taking someone as young as you away for such a great quest, so we did try recasting Pundlaboa for other uishanoles of the royal blooded Veshaels in your world. However, no matter how specifically I worded the spell for finding other uishanoles that weren't you, no light formed guiding us to someone else. Therefore, that means you're the only living uishanole. As for the other uishanoles, they've likely existed in the past, are currently dead or haven't been born yet."

Feeling as if she's losing the battle with her self-control, Phoebe yells, "Well-well can't the spell on the Vinston Scepter be undone and ha-have someone else u-use it?!"

Phoebe is close to a full blown panic attack, and the yuets stare at her uneasily.

"Please, calm yourself Qelphy," Cernin pleads. "That would be next to impossible. The spells cast onto both the Vinston and Monston scepters are permanent, so no matter what, you're the only one we can rely on."

Phoebe struggles to control her rampaging emotions as tears begin to seep from her eyes. She attempts to figure out other ways to get out of completing this extremely undesirable task. "Well…Wh-what if someone did what Gaphanagon did…except with…light magic, making that yuet powerful enough to f-fight off the Xeffizens?!"

"We cannot do that." Cernin says. "Ever since Gaphanagon's defeat the devouring of magic, both good and evil, has been banned in Yuetsion. It's just too big a risk to ask someone to do that for us, no matter how good their intentions might be. And besides, taking care of a giant yuet would have very bad effects on all the regular yuets in many ways."

This can't be! There's no way out of this! What am I going to do?!

"Please! Let me go home! Let me go home!"

"I can't! Look, we're very sorry we brought you here against your will, but we need you! Your part in all of this is too important. We'll definitely let you go home as soon as you've completed your quest to destroy the Monston Scepter or at least tried using the Vinston Scepter, if it doesn't end up working for you."

"No please! Mother! Father! Wake me up from this nightmare!" Phoebe screams. The symptoms associated with her autism are becoming uncontrollable and she starts to hit her head with her hand as she cries, which is something she hasn't done in several years.

Hezkale backs nervously away from her with a look of bewilderment in his eyes.

"Can someone please calm her down?!" Cernin says.

Yorgo hurriedly grabs hold of Phoebe's wrist. The touch of his reptilian skin shocks her. She cringes trying to pull herself free from his grasp.

"There, there Qelphy," Yorgo says.

Unable to put up with Yorgo anymore, she bites his hand, causing him to wince in pain, unhanding her.

Phoebe instinctively sprints back toward the way she came in. Mysty races after her. She shoves the door open with all her weight and she and Mysty squeeze through it, escaping into the hallway. She runs in what she hopes is the direction of her room.

"Qelphy, wait!" Hilmina calls out rushing out of the room.

Racing down the hallways, Phoebe barges past any yuets standing in her way. Finally arriving at the safety of her bedroom, she scrambles inside, waits a couple seconds for Mysty to race in and slams the door tightly behind them. Mysty looks up at her in shock. Phoebe leans back against the door and slides down to the ground, her breath coming in shaky ragged gasps. Mysty rests her paws against Phoebe's leg, meowing reassuringly. "I take back my wish about ever running away into a fantasy world! Now I'll never see mom and dad again…Never!" Mysty's ears droop down and she meows in a depressed tone. As tears of hysteria trail down her cheeks, Phoebe envisions blurred images of her parents. For a moment she feels like she can touch them, like they're in the room with her, but then they fade away and she's left alone once again.

Chapter 7

Phoebe absentmindedly pinches the rich fabric of her bedding as she sits cross-legged, listening to the barely audible strains of music coming from outside her windows.

Mysty snuggles cozily by her side, letting out a leisurely yawn, and Phoebe rolls onto her back and watches as the sunbeams dance along the drapery until darkness overtakes the room. Thin moonlight slivers slice through the gaps in the linen drapes, casting shimmery light. Unexpectedly, new streams of light appear everywhere and Phoebe finds herself strangely attracted to the spectacular display, which reminds her of stardust or the Northern Lights. The light-streams seem to be attracted to the chandeliers' crystals, as well as her bedside lamps, which causes them to glow. The more intently she focuses her attention, the more she realizes she's seen these light formations before. They look exactly like the auroras flowing within the mirror-packed aisles of her dream.

"Mysty!" Phoebe whispers, sitting up. "Are you seeing this?!"

Mysty meows.

"I-I-I've seen this before! These lights were in my dreams…I mean if they were dreams." Mysty stares up at Phoebe with a curious expression. "If it wasn't a dream and if this right now isn't a dream, then maybe that mirrored maze was a part of Yuetsion too. But how would I even get transported from one location to a completely different one if I was never dreaming? And if this and the mirrored maze are one oversized dream after all…then what's keeping me from waking up?"

Mysty tilts her head questioningly, mewling.

"Hmm, well I know one thing: the mirror chambers and Yuetsion definitely have a connection, especially when that mirror area kind of foretold me about Princess Vehilia and the Vinston Scepter and…maybe these light streams too." Phoebe gazes down at Mysty, who's starting to look cross-eyed. "Well, whatever the whole situation is…I still miss mom and dad." Disheartened, Phoebe holds her legs up to her body. "I really need them."

Mysty mews in a dismayed tone twice, resting her paws on Phoebe's foot. "Yeah, you really need them too. At least we still have each other right?"

Mysty purrs, rubbing herself against Phoebe. "I love you too Mysty."

Phoebe waves her arm curiously through the streams of light. Mysty too shakes her paws, and the streams swish around as if pulled by invisible air currents. The lights seem to flow right through their bodies. Looking back at the chandelier, Phoebe lifts her necklace up. Even her amethyst gems glow.

"Ace! My amethyst gems are glowing too! These light streams even enhanced my necklace! Just where did these come from? Maybe…they only appear at night? Or…"

Reaching over to the bedside table, Phoebe turns on the crystal lamp, unveiling a bright glowing white gem that illuminates the room. As she watches, she can see the light streams grow dim as they grow closer to the gem, to the point of being nearly invisible. The crystal lampshade and her amethyst gems are starting to lose their radiance too.

"Oh…" Phoebe says, scratching her chin with fascination. "So these beautiful lights can only be seen in the dark and can't even make crystals glow when bright. In that case…" She turns the lamp's knob, effectively darkening the room. "Better." Sighing pensively, she gives Mysty's cheeks a vigorous rub. The tiny kitten replies immediately with a vibrating purr. As astounding as the streams of light are, she's bored at being sequestered in her room. She feels the need to converse with someone, even if it's only a cat.

"Oh Mysty, as amazing as this light show is, I can't keep myself trapped in this room forever. Perhaps it's finally time to stop being so afraid and…I guess try to be braver around the yuets, dream or not. But will they still accept me for who I am after I acted so foolishly? Maybe they'll judge me, labeling me as being too self-centered and a helpless cry-baby."

Phoebe holds her cat at eye level. She can clearly see her reflection in the golden orbs of Mysty's eyes, and it's as if she's looking into her own soul. "What do you think?" Mysty mews reassuringly as she reaches out a paw and flicks Phoebe's bangs playfully, making her giggle. "No, you're right Mysty. They don't seem to be the judgmental type of people…or yuets. At least they don't act like it."

Phoebe's stomach releases a grumble, reminding her she hasn't eaten anything all day. Mysty meows impatiently too.

"You think it's safe enough for us to leave and eat?" Phoebe asks. Mysty nods her head. "Alright, I'll take your word for it." As she stands up, she attempts to flatten out the wrinkles on the bedspread. "Come on girl—let's go find a kitchen." Mysty rushes excitedly to the door with her bushy tail sticking straight up as it sways gently to and fro. Phoebe smothers a laugh. The movement of Mysty's tail reminds her of the movements of Yorgo's tail when he was escorting her to see Cernin.

Phoebe takes a deep breath as she pushes open the door and wanders out into the hallway with the streams of light flowing out after them. The blue crystals on the walls glow with a dim phosphorescence. Set inside intricately designed glass holders edged in pure silver, they and the streams of light deliver just enough light for Phoebe to see by. Glancing in both directions, Phoebe lets go of the breath she didn't even realize she had been holding. No yuets appear to be anywhere in sight, which makes her feel more comfortable with roaming down the passage. After playing a short game of eeny, meeny, miney, mo in her head, Phoebe elects to head down the hallway to her left. She pauses frequently to make sure no one is following her. She's so intent on her quest that she fails to see the rich detailing of the paneling on the walls.

Light spills into the hallway from an alcove up ahead. With her back against the wall, Phoebe creeps quietly forward until she's close enough to the break in the wall, signaling the entrance of the alcove. Peering around the corner, she confirms the source of the light is a delicately carved crystal, set inside a large glass holder. It's similar to the ones in the hallway, but far more elaborate and twice as big. It hangs directly above a door that is slightly ajar. Faint voices can be heard coming from inside the room. Taking great pains to conceal her presence, Phoebe silently tiptoes up to the door and peers inside. In the dim light, she can make out two figures that seem to be having a rather serious conversation. Straining her ears, she's finally able to identify the voices of the speakers. *It's Hilmina and Cernin.* She blocks the front of the door with her foot to prevent Mysty from wandering in.

"You can't make her do this," Hilmina exclaims. The agitation in her voice is clearly emphasized by her hand gestures. "She's way too young for a job like this!"

"But, Hilmina, we need her specifically 'because' she's Princess Vehilia's uishanole!" Cernin says.

They're talking about me. She has a sickening feeling that whenever she hears the word 'uishanole', it's always going to be in reference to her. At this time, the name sounds rather insulting, as if it's being used by someone, possibly a bully, who doesn't know what to call someone and ends up making up his own insulting name by pulling a word out of thin air.

"But she's just a child. At the most she can't be any older than twelve." Hilmina thumps her tail loudly on the floor for emphasis.

I'm thirteen years old, but that's close enough.

"I understand that…" Cernin says. "Hilmina, you must be aware that I'm against it as much as you are. But we really have no other alternative."

"Are you sure there are no other uishanoles who are at least a few years older?"

"I'm sorry Hilmina, but the magic proved to us she's most definitely the only uishanole and the Pundlaboa spell never lies. Besides, remember why you and Yorgo joined my group in the first place?"

Hilmina's shadowy head droops. "I know. As much as I don't approve of what you're doing, it's probably the only way we can save her."

"If we send the uishanole back now, we won't have any hope of rescuing your daughter. I'm sorry, but it's the truth."

Phoebe is startled by their conversation. *Her daughter? Hilmina and Yorgo are parents? Well, I guess that explains*

Hilmina's motherly attitude, but I wonder what happened to their daughter.

"Just promise me the uishanole will remain safe," Hilmina says.

"As long as the Xeffizens never find out what we're up to, everything should run smoothly and the uishanole should remain safe."

Their agitated voices grow louder as they begin to walk towards the door. Realizing she might be discovered, Phoebe silently gasps, as she reaches down and picks up Mysty. She ducks behind the door mere seconds before it's pushed open. When the door swings open, she tries to make herself as invisible as possible. Still deep in conversation, Hilmina and Cernin don't have any clue Phoebe is hidden behind the door. The pair makes their way quickly out of the alcove and down the hallway. After a few moments Phoebe peers around the corner of the alcove, watching the swaying tails of the two yuets fade farther into the distance.

Phoebe breathes a sigh of relief. "That was close."

With Mysty taking the lead and her stomach still rumbling loudly; Phoebe resumes her search. As they proceed down the hallway, Phoebe goes over the conversation she had overheard. *What could Hilmina's daughter possibly have to do with me being a uishanole and what else haven't they told me?*

The hallway finally dead-ends and Phoebe is left standing in front of a set of open double doors. Phoebe's nose picks up all sorts of tantalizing aromas coming from within its depths. The room has a rather inviting feel to it. A magnificently carved wooden table takes up the majority of the room, dozens of chairs with decorative cushioned seats and elaborately carved backs have been placed in precise positions around the table and moonlight pours into the room through the seven stained glass windows encompassing it: five on the wall directly opposite the entrance and two others facing each other from opposing walls. Each window seems to depict a different historical scene. The dark paneling on the walls provides a welcoming contrast to the off-white drapes hanging on each side of the windows. Exquisite crystal glasses are placed in front of each chair, and the overall grandeur of the room leaves Phoebe with the impression this room has seen its fair share of visiting royalty.

    Approaching one end of the table, Phoebe spies a large silver platter filled with a variety of colourful foods. Hoping the food is edible she glances down at her still-rumbling stomach. The food looks familiar, but at the same time not so familiar. There are the usual cupcakes, donuts, tarts and squares, but there are also some items on the platter which are completely foreign to her, like a pyramid-shaped dessert loaded with frosting. *Hopefully no one would mind or even judge me if I take a few of these. I'm starving after all. Wait…Who am I kidding? They consider me as their rescuer. They would let me eat if I needed to or they should at least.*

    Looking around carefully to see if anyone is watching, Phoebe takes one of the cupcake-like treats and takes a nibble. An explosion of flavours sends her taste buds into overload. Eyes widening at its incredible sweetness, she quickly takes another bite. The second bite seems to be even more delectable than the first. Quickly shoving the rest of the cupcake into her mouth, she uses the back of her hand to wipe away any crumbs. Mysty rubs up against Phoebe's leg and lets out a frustrated meow, as if to remind Phoebe she's hungry too. Studying the treats on the platter,

Phoebe chooses a couple which look rather bun-like in nature and don't have a lot of icing or sugar on top of them. She puts them down in front of Mysty and the kitten immediately pounces on them. Large rumbling purrs can soon be heard as the cat happily munches on her food. Feeling extremely ecstatic to have finally found food, Phoebe eats the sweets at a rapid pace.

"I see ya love to eat."

Startled, Phoebe whirls around and almost drops the food in her hand. Yorgo smiles, with his arms folded, leaning against the door frame of the entrance. His dark dress shirt is unbuttoned and a cream coloured shirt peaks out from underneath. The belt pulled tightly through the loops on his dark brown pants fails to contain his rather large tummy. Phoebe was so intent on eating she hadn't noticed Yorgo entering into the room. She's suddenly aware of the bun sticking out of her mouth and blushes as she shoves it fully into her mouth. Yorgo's sudden appearance should be making her feel very uncomfortable, but she feels more embarrassed over being caught with her hand in the proverbial cookie jar.

Yorgo steps up to her and Phoebe can see the laugh lines radiating outwards from his mouth. His yellowish green eyes hold a glint of amusement in them, as he quickly inspects her. "You eat almost as fast as I," Yorgo laughs. His cream coloured shirt is noticeably tighter around his midsection.

Phoebe blushes and frowns at him. *You have a lot of guts to say that to a girl.*

She looks at the hand she had chomped back in Cernin's lab. Oddly, there seems to be no evidence of any bite marks. In fact, it's as if nothing had ever happened. Reptilian skin must be extremely tough.

"I'm sorry," she blurts out.

"Sorry?" Yorgo asks. He looks at what Phoebe is looking at. "Oh! That's all right. It didn't really hurt my hand that much when you bit it. In fact, it was only a pinch. I don't get hurt that easily. I guess I kind of made a big deal outta it because I was shocked that you bit me." Yorgo rubs the back of his head. "By the way, do you like my food?"

Phoebe points at the platter of food. "Yours?"

"Why yes. I baked all of the food you see here. I'm a professional baker and chef. I used to work in the royal kitchens before my family and I moved," he explains.

"You cooked for r-royalty?" Phoebe asks with amazement. Thinking about the tastes of his food, they definitely taste fit for royalty. *His baking is very good after all; maybe even better quality than my mom's.*

"Oh yes Qelphy. I don't mean ta brag, but I used to get endless compliments from royalty all over the world, especially from Princess Vehilia."

"You knew Princess Vehilia?!"

"I sure did. As far as I know, she loved my cooking more than anyone." He chuckles a tad. "Speaking of which, funny story, it's all my fault fer getting Princess Vehilia obsessed over yether cakes, thanks to my homemade recipe."

Phoebe stiffens, staring at him, unable to express herself or get the words to soar out.

"What?" Phoebe asks, testing herself if she listened correctly.

"I said my homemade yether cakes caused Princess Vehilia to become outrageously attached ta them. I may have accidentally made her selfish in a way, but all was good. In fact, I wish you had seen her charge through the crowds like a boulder the instant my yether cakes were set out." Phoebe is dumbfounded upon hearing his story. His story flashes her back to the dream scene she witnessed, with Princess Vehilia changing from formal to insanity just at the mention of yether cakes.

Looking down at his belly, Yorgo gives it a pat and laughs. "Even I can't resist my own cooking." He looks over at Phoebe. "Um, is something wrong Qelphy?"

"Oh," Phoebe says, shaking her head. "It's nothing."

"Are ya sure?"

"Yeah um…I'm just…dazed…I need food."

"Well, a chef can't let anyone starve. Help yourself to the food on the table. There's plenty of it. Let me know if there's anything else I can fix up for you."

Hmmm, what would a typical yuet eat? Phoebe thinks about the one food she cannot live without. Is it possible the cuisine of these strange creatures includes the tantalizingly delicious treat known as chocolate?

"Chocolate?"

"What's…choc-o-late?" Yorgo asks.

Phoebe reels backwards in shock. If Yorgo, a self-proclaimed baker and chef, doesn't know anything about chocolate, does that mean it doesn't exist in this world? The thought of living in a world without her favourite treat leaves her feeling lightheaded, close to the point of fainting.

"I'm not sure I know what chocolate is, but I can definitely fix up somethin for you if you like. Perhaps you would enjoy one of Hilmina's favourite dishes," Yorgo offers.

Still focusing on the lack of chocolate in this strange world, Phoebe smiles politely and shakes her head. She points to the plate of goodies no longer heaped as high as it was mere moments earlier.

"Are you sayin that plateful is enough for you?"

At a momentary loss for words, Phoebe nods her head in acknowledgment.

"All right den, let me just grab a little something too and I'll be on my way." Yorgo grabs three items off the platter. Popping one of them into his mouth, he chews it slowly before swallowing. "If you need anything, I'll be in the kitchen next door." He waddles out of the room.

After waiting several minutes to make sure Yorgo isn't coming back, Phoebe returns her attention back to the plate of goodies. Although she's still struggling to wrap her head around the fact there's no chocolate, the ongoing rumbling of her stomach serves as a reminder there are plenty of other treats for her to try. She picks up something which looks suspiciously like a blueberry muffin and takes a huge bite out of it. It tastes so good she quickly wolfs down the rest of it and reaches for another one. The deliciousness of the food helps to ease her worries to the point she stops thinking about her extremely realistic dream. *Ace, ace and ace!*

A short time later she concludes she has had enough. A small burp escapes from her mouth and she breathes out a sigh of satisfaction. Now having fulfilled the requests of her stomach, it's time to return to her explorations. Heading back into the hallway, Phoebe pauses momentarily to allow her eyes to readjust to the dimness of the crystals lighting the passageway. With her eyes properly adjusted, she proceeds down the path with Mysty trailing along behind her.

The duo resumes their explorations for about half an hour without seeing anyone else, until they come across a portion of the hallway with a railing. Hearing voices from down below Phoebe peers over the railing. One floor down, she can make out the red colourations of a Kume and the blue colourations of a Veshael. Judging by their feminine features and the fact they're both wearing dresses, Phoebe feels it's safe to come to the conclusion they're female. Both yuets are deep in conversation with each other. She hears them talking and giggling about subjects like male yuets they're attracted to and what their "gorgeous guys" have done and said to them. Phoebe feels as if she's back in school hearing the girls talking about boys and the boys talking about girls. *Huh, I guess yuets have similar minds to humans. That should make talking to them easier at least.* A small speck of dust flies up Phoebe's nose, triggering a violent sneeze. The yuets gawk up at her in surprise, but before they can ask her what she's doing, she pulls back from the railing and ducks out of sight.

"How about we explore a couple more halls and then we head back to our room," she asks. Mysty agrees. They pass by a room with a door slightly cracked open. Squinting, Phoebe tries to see what's inside, but the lack of light within is making it next to impossible to see much of anything. "No one's inside. Do you think we should go in?" Mysty meows as if to say she wants to see what's inside. "All right, one quick peak. But at the first sign of trouble, we're leaving."

Pushing the door open to enter into the room, she discovers a faintly radiant crystal lamp sitting on a nearby desk. Running her hand along the wall behind it, she soon finds the knob and turns it on. The iridescent glow of the crystal emits a bright amount of light. Looking around, Phoebe finds herself inside a bedroom roughly the same size as the one she has slept in. A four poster bed takes centre stage in between two vast stained glass windows against one wall. Crisp white sheets are folded back over top of a crimson comforter and pillow cases in the same crimson hue sit at the head of the bed. The two stained glass windows take up almost the entire height of the wall. The images depicted on them show scenes of a battle. Two crossed swords hang on the wall at the head of the bed. *Does a swordsman sleep here?* Mysty leaps onto the bed and playfully pounces around on its blankets.

Looking back at the finely carved wooden desk near the door, Phoebe's curiosity gets the better of her. She begins opening drawers trying to find answers for whom this room belongs to. In the top drawer, she finds a jumble of strange items she's nowhere near being able to identify. Unfortunately, because everything is so foreign to her and she has no idea exactly what it is she's looking for, she's forced to close the drawer in defeat. Opening the second drawer down, she lets out a sigh of exasperation at coming across yet another pile of unidentifiable objects. As she's about to close the drawer and leave the room, Phoebe catches sight of a small case partially hidden beneath a piece of cloth. It looks suspiciously like the type of item one would bring home from a jewelry store. Picking it up, she opens it and is awestruck by what she finds inside. A beautiful golden ring with strange scrollwork and symbols etched all along the outside of the band. The facets of the luminous violet diamond-like gem set in its exact centre wink in the light coming from the lamp. Jewelry-wise, she has never seen anything quite so beautiful before. It's an especially unique find since the gem happens to be her favourite colour. Hoping the owner of the ring won't be angry with her, she slips it onto the ring finger of her left hand. A perfect fit! Twisting the ring around on her finger, she admires the beauty of the diamond and caresses her fingers across the scrollwork etched on the smooth surface of the band. A closer examination leads her to believe the etching on the band isn't just a design, but a series of words written in a strange language or code which definitely isn't Brimcolf lettering since she can't understand what it says.

"Ace," Phoebe says.

"Hey! What are you doing in here?" The lack of sound in the room, up to this point, allows the speaker's voice to echo off the walls.

Phoebe whirls around, horrified to be caught snooping through someone else's belongings. Standing behind her is a surprised Hezkale, hands on his hips, with his purple mincy, Riddy, preening himself and sitting on his shoulder. He eyes the ring Phoebe is still wearing on her finger. Blushing, Phoebe quickly pulls it off and sets the ring and case on top of the desk. Fearing what she'll see in Hezkale's eyes and what judgmental thoughts are radiating in his mind, she avoids all eye contact with him as she heads towards the door with the intention of leaving the room. Hezkale quickly moves to block her escape and raises his hands. His purple eyes seem to bore right through her.

"Oh wait, sorry. I didn't mean to scare you. I was just wondering what you're doing in here. Not that I'm mad, but surprised."

"E-e-exploring," Phoebe can feel her cheeks heating up and knows they are turning an intense shade of red.

"Exploring, huh? I guess that's what I get for not locking my door." His face takes on a look of concern as he glances over at Phoebe. She can see a hint of amusement in his greenish purple eyes. "Are you feeling any better after that bombshell Cernin and the others dropped on you earlier? It can't be easy, knowing you are tasked with such a difficult responsibility."

Unsure of how to respond, Phoebe drops her gaze to the floor. Dream or not, she has yet to come to terms with the idea of being Princess Vehilia's uishanole and about her role in upcoming events, but she nods anyways.

Hezkale picks up the ring from the desk and looks thoughtfully over at Phoebe. "Do you really like this ring?"

Phoebe can feel the heat rising even higher in her cheeks as she smiles and nods her head. Gesturing for Phoebe to put out her hand, he gently places the ring into the palm of her hand.

"You know, it actually suits you very well...If you'd like, you may wear it until it's time for you to return home to your world."

Phoebe is bewildered by his surprising gesture. "Th-thank…you." She carefully places the ring back on her finger and smiles.

"It looks very beautiful on you," Hezkale says.

"Thank you very much," she says, slipping it on. She gives him a shy glance. No boy has ever given her jewelry before. He seems to be intent on cultivating a friendship with her. Perhaps she has misjudged him.

Hezkale's gaze fixates on one particular spot on the wall. Phoebe determines by the look of concentration in his eyes he must be thinking about something. Riddy leans his head in close to Hezkale's ear and lets out chirps of encouragement. It's as if the two of them are having a silent discussion with each other. After a few seconds, Hezkale focuses his gaze back to Phoebe.

"Qelphy, have you been shown the tower's garden yet?"

Nodding her head, Phoebe hopes he's talking about the same garden Hilmina had taken her to earlier in the day.

"Have you seen it at night yet?"

Pausing for a moment at this unexpected question, Phoebe can only shake her head. *Would the garden look that much different at night?*

"You haven't? Great, you are in for a special treat. Follow me and I'll lead the way to the garden." Hezkale swiftly turns to leave the room, causing Riddy to lose his balance. The bird squawks his displeasure and ruffles up his feathers in annoyance.

Hezkale holds the door wide open for her. Phoebe treads out of his room with Mysty leaping off the bed and following by her side. Hezkale moves up to stand beside her so he can walk by her side. Riddy flies off Hezkale's shoulder and lands on Phoebe's. His feathers fluff up, as if he has been blow dried.

"Well look at that. When he fluffs up his feathers it means he likes you," Hezkale says.

Phoebe chuckles at Riddy's cuteness.

"I like him too," Phoebe says.

Mysty meows in a jealous tone and stands on her hind legs, indicating she wants to be held. Phoebe picks the kitten up, cradling her in her arms and making her purr cheerfully. Riddy flies back onto Hezkale's shoulder, straightens out his feathers and whistles happily.

"Right this way," Hezkale says.

Hezkale leads Phoebe through a maze of hallways and down a few flights of stairs. Phoebe keeps her attention on Hezkale for the majority of the time, and not just because of his swaying tail. Normally, she doesn't stare at strangers, but he's been so kind that she just can't help it. Is this what it feels like to have a friend?

Chapter 8

Hezkale leads Phoebe through the Hiljin Tower's labyrinthine halls, Riddy chirping happily on his shoulder, before stopping abruptly at a set of closed double doors—the same ones Hilmina brought her to earlier. Phoebe smiles in anticipation, a heavy-eyed Mysty stuffed underneath one arm.

"Close your eyes please," Hezkale says.

I don't see any point in closing my eyes since I've already been here, but I guess I'll do it for him.

Phoebe obliges and hears the faint creak of hinges as he shoves open the doors.

"All right, now take about seven steps forward," Hezkale says.

Phoebe takes a few steps. The floor texture transitions from a smooth surface to rough, sharp stone and finally to the dry dustiness of a dirt pathway.

"You can open your eyes now." Hezkale says.

Opening her eyes, Phoebe is transfixed by the stunning display before her. It's completely different from her daylight visit; only even better. With the expected swarms of streams of light, the plants she had found so astonishing earlier in the day are even more beautiful without the sun shining on them. A kaleidoscope of phosphorescence spreads through the air. From their stems to their blossoms each plant glows a distinctly different colour. Even the crystals and the other minerals in the garden are shimmering luminously and the crystal fountains make the water glitter as vividly as the plants and minerals. The streams of light seem to hover over everything, intensifying the glow of any surface they come in contact with—especially the minerals. Gazing up at the night sky, she becomes even more bedazzled, witnessing the gorgeous displays of the multiple different stone and ringed gas moons of differing colours and sizes. She can even spot a few distant nebulas. *There must be absolutely no light pollution in Yuetsion's atmosphere!* She looks down at Mysty, now wide awake, who appears to be mesmerized. The little orange tabby immediately leaps off Phoebe's arm and wanders about, playfully waving her paws at the streams of light.

Curious, Phoebe glances down at her amethyst necklace and the ring Hezkale gave her. The gems embedded in the jewelry are glowing. *Such beauty! I wonder what it is about the night time or the darkness of Yuetsion that makes the streams of light appear and make all the minerals glow, along with the plants too!*

"Ace!" Phoebe says.

She turns to look at Hezkale.

"Behold the outdoors of Yuetsion at night! Beautiful, isn't it?"

"Hezkale, this is amazing! I've never seen so much light in one place before!"

Skipping out onto the grass, she twirls happily. She's not surprised when the streams of light flow around with her, too. *Is this what Heaven is like?*

"This is my favourite time of the day to come here," Hezkale says.

"Are we-we alone?"

"Most likely, hardly anyone ever comes here anymore." He pauses as if abruptly remembering something. "I guess it's because this was Princess Vehilia's favourite place to come whenever her family was busy doing research in the labs. I think it brings back too many unwanted memories. But it hasn't stopped me from coming back."

"Yeah..." Phoebe sighs. "I just love looking at these l-lights."

"Do you have anything like this back in your world?" Hezkale asks.

"Well...there are the Northern Lights," Phoebe says. "You can-can only see them up in the north, except these lights seem to only be seen anywhere that's dark." Phoebe's curiosity grows. "Say... Hezkale, what exactly are these lights?"

"Oh, they're lights that are made up of tiny particles called qwitsuls," Hezkale says.

"Quit-sulls? What are they?"

"They're extremely powerful micro spirits. They create Yuetsion's magic and power the machinery and vehicles of this world."

Phoebe is shocked.

"You mean…all of this is Yuetsion's magic and its elect-electricity and they're all made of micro spirits?" Phoebe asks

"That's correct."

"Amazing…Yuetsion is a world of magic and technology. So…would qwitsuls be more like…a form of energy, a living energy?"

"Exactly."

"But then why…why did you and Cernin call it magic when it's energy?"

"We yuets address the qwitsuls as magic when we use them for that purpose and energy when used as technology, but really altogether…they're just a very powerful living energy."

"Oh…fascinating…but…what happens to them when it's bright?"

"Nothing happens to them. They're still flowing around everywhere. It's just that their glow can only be seen in the dark."

"Oh, I see," Phoebe says, gazing back up at the flowing qwitsuls. "Qwitsuls…Micro spirits…I wonder what they look like up close."

"You can see how they look through specific crystals. They can make great magnifying glasses."

"Really?"

"Definitely." Hezkale bends down with Riddy whistling and flapping his wings on his shoulder and picks up a glowing green gem from the ground. He hands it to her. "Here, observe through this one closely. It's the kind I normally use whenever I want a better view of the qwitsuls."

Phoebe holds the mineral up to her eye and squints. Tiny, multi-coloured dots float inside. She identifies the dots as microscopic, iridescent, transparent beings, appearing to be made entirely out of perfectly carved crystals, floating around within it and they all seem to be sleeping.

"Wow!" Phoebe says with her eyes widening, holding the crystal away and looking closely into it again. "They're like tiny glimmering crystal beings."

"That's not all. If you listen carefully, you can also hear them sing."

"They sing too?"

"Oh yes, they flow through your ears the whole time, so all you have to do is ignore all the other sounds and focus on the qwitsuls to hear them. Try plugging your ears."

"Hmm…" Phoebe replaces the gem, which Mysty rubs her cheek against, and plugs her ears with her fingers to shut out all the external sounds. To her surprise, she begins to hear a mysterious, harmonious rhythm, sounding closest to heavenly musical voices, forming a slow-paced celestial choir. It's so peaceful, calming and mystifying.

"I can hear them…" Phoebe says. "Their music sounds…so soothing with their…angelic voices."

"You heard right."

"I never thought I would witness something as other worldly as qwitsuls," Phoebe says, unplugging her ears. She gets confused, remembering the magic coming out of Cernin's scepter. "But…I thought the magic came from scepters like Cernin's and I would im-im-imagine the machinery would generate their own electricity. How does it work, if it comes from the qwitsuls instead?"

"That's easy," Hezkale says. "You see, qwitsuls can flow through everything because they have very, very, very little matter when unused, just enough matter for flowing air to control their movements. In fact, they have even less matter than air. When they're cast as spells or flow through specific materials, that's when they gain more matter. When it comes to qwitsul magic usage, we use crystals because the qwitsuls have always been more attracted to minerals than any other material. They compress when absorbed, which you can probably already tell since the minerals of this world glow the most out of everything, some brighter and some dimmer, depending on how many qwitsuls each crystal's material attracts or how thin or thick their material is. We use the crystals that can contain the most qwitsuls for scepters and the nice thing about them is that their material is generally too thick to emit a bright glow to bother your eyes. You cast the qwitsuls in a magical form from your scepter's crystal orb, emptying out all the qwitsuls within it, while at the same time new unused qwitsuls from the outside are reabsorbed back into the crystal up to the maximum amount it can contain. Well, except for with the Vinston and Monston Scepters of course—those two can contain practically endless amounts."

"Wow..." Phoebe says. "So...so that's how Cernin's illusion worked. It was made of qwitsuls...How do qwitsuls have little matter and then just gain more matter though?"

"Qwitsuls are immensely powerful with numerous wondrous abilities. They're powerful enough to adjust their own matter when needed. They don't seem like much when floating about in the air, but when instructed right, they're phenomenal."

"Amazing...but...I could see the qwitsuls in the light when Cernin used them as illusions."

"Qwitsuls can be seen in the light when large enough amounts of them are compressed together, especially when used for spell-casting."

"Oh..."

"As for the machinery," Hezkale continues, "they have built in mechanisms that suck billions of qwitsuls into the machinery and transport them throughout the tubes and wiring of the machines. The tubes and wires contain mineral material that automatically makes them transform into functioning qwitsul energy with increased matter when flowing through them and entrapping their power within the machinery until they lose their charge, making the machinery run smoothly."

"Amazing!" Phoebe says. "A world without electric bills!"

"Huh?"

"Oh, nothing. So, the plants are glowing from...the qwitsuls too?"

"Oh yes, most of the plants absorb them a lot like the stone minerals, only they can't hold enough to be useful for weaponry or machinery. It's enough to make them glow beautifully in the dark, though. Even some of Yuetsion's creatures have bodies made of material that attracts qwitsuls, making their skin, eyes, insides or feathers glow too—especially the nocturnal ones." Hezkale plucks an aqua glowing leaf off a nearby branch. "See?"

Phoebe takes the leaf from him. To her surprise, she can see the qwitsuls flowing into and through the lines of the leaves and back out repeatedly, making it gleam.

"They really are flowing into the leaves. They're amazing!" Phoebe says. "If the qwitsuls can get absorbed…into crystals and plants, would they absorb into us as well?"

"Well, not exactly, they flow through us no problem, but nothing about Veshael bodies attracts them. I'm pretty sure your body doesn't attract them that easily either, which you can pretty much tell by us not glowing. Though some yuets speculate that as you cast qwitsuls from scepters or any other weapon that requires them, some of the qwitsuls from the casting process get stuck and contained within your body and even your spirit, which is possible seeing how qwitsuls themselves are spirits too."

Phoebe raises an eyebrow. "How could they do that?"

"Well," Hezkale says waving his finger around like a poised professor, "in order for the qwitsuls to understand your instructions on how to be cast, they rapidly flow from the crystal, through your scepter's mast and into your body, as they gain matter. Once in your body, they flow straight into your mind, which is a part of your spirit, back all the way into the scepter's crystal and instantly cast out from it the way you want them to...with the possible exception of the qwitsuls that got stuck to your innards and spirit during the process of course. What's even more extraordinary is that during the process of the qwitsuls following your mind's instructions, the qwitsuls getting cast out develop minds and intentions exactly like your own, getting out of their constant neutral mindsets. Their neutral mindedness comes again when their power's drained."

"Really? All qwitsul spells make qwitsuls develop your exact mind?"

"Well, most for sure. Some qwitsul spells don't change the qwitsuls' mindsets like Pundlaboa. For that qwitsul spell, they'd have to remain their original omniscient selves in order to properly guide you to whatever you seek. If they develop your mind, they'll only know as much as what you seek as you do, making them useless for qwitsul spells like that."

"My gosh...they're omniscient too? These qwitsuls sound...marvelous..."

"Oh they are Qelphy. They are."

"But...about them sticking to your innards and spirit...wouldn't they lose their charge and flow...out of your body and spirit after gaining matter, if they got stuck to them during a spell casting process?"

"Mmm...not quite. They may have gained matter during the process, but they wouldn't have their power fully drained since they weren't fully cast. We yuets would imagine they'd maintain within you for a good long while until you properly spell-cast them out, using your body like you would with scepters, but of course the qwitsuls your body collected wouldn't compare to the amount an ordinary scepter's crystal collects...well, maybe unless it's the Vinston Scepter or Monston Scepter you've been using."

"Oh okay...I guess that makes sense."

"Another way for your body to definitely contain qwitsuls is that you cast them and give them additional matter everlastingly with everlasting spells and then eat them like Gaphanagon did, but trust me, you'd never want to do that, otherwise you'd break the largest law of Yuetsion and end up being a monster like Gaphanagon."

"Uh-uh, I won't go there." Phoebe quivers at the thought. "If qwitsuls are flowing through us now...could we cast them through our...f-fingers?"

"Oh yes, we can cast them without the help of other weapons, but only by a pinch. Watch this." Hezkale holds out his hand. "Jephimum, flow to my fingertips." His fingertips' skin and nails glimmer with multiple colourations. "See?"

Phoebe's jaw drops. Riddy hops and sidesteps along Hezkale's arm to his hand and nosily stares at his shining fingertips as he tries to nibble on them, making Hezkale chuckle a touch. "You try."

Phoebe looks at her hand and concentrates hard on it. "Jephimum, flow to my fingertips." Her fingertips begin shining like Hezkale's. "Oh my gosh! This is really happening!"

"I was as amazed as you, when I was taught about the qwitsuls' abilities. They really know how to keep this planet alive."

Phoebe takes her mind off her hands, ceasing their luminosity and Hezkale mimics her action. With a disappointed chirp, Riddy stops chewing on Hezkale's fingers and moves back onto his shoulder.

"Fascinating…" Phoebe says, rubbing her fingers, "so that's how they respond to our commands. And…is using specific material that triggers the qwitsuls to gain matter and use their power for things like machinery an alternate way of communicating with them?"

"Undeniably," Hezkale says. "It's a way of instructing them without using your mind for communication."

"So altogether it's like…the qwitsuls take care of everyone here in Yuetsion."

"Yes, in fact, yuets believe that we and the qwitsuls are taking care of each other."

"Like a family."

"Yes, exactly!"

"But…where do these qwitsuls come from? Surely they come from somewhere."

"They do actually. They come from underground, through the planet's surface," Hezkale says, thumping his foot against the dirt.

"From underground?"

"Yes, endless amounts of them."

"But, what if…what if there will come a time when this planet runs out of qwitsuls? What will happen then?"

"That actually won't ever happen because as new qwitsuls come from underground, the used dim ones, which are the ones that have used up their powers from being cast or powering machinery, sink back down."

"Really?"

"Really. We believe there's something deep below the planet's surface that's possibly regenerating every qwitsul's power, which we named The Qwitsul Regenerator. New qwitsuls rise up from underground, they get used for spell casting or technology, they become dim and weak, they sink back down underground and finally, they become new and powerful again and rise from underground again, no matter how many qwitsuls get used up every day. We yuets call it The Qwitsul Cycle. Therefore, qwitsuls are eternal."

"That's a miracle! What regenerates the qwitsuls?"

"Don't know. No one has ever discovered what The Qwitsul Regenerator is yet because it's too deep underground for us to reach, no matter how far down we dig. Cernin would really go wild if The Qwitsul Regenerator ever gets discovered."

Phoebe and Hezkale laugh. "Wait," Phoebe says, "but if qwitsuls need recharging after being cast, then how do those 'everlasting' qwitsul spells work? Wouldn't those qwitsuls used everlastingly need recharging too?"

"Oh the qwitsuls used in everlasting spells definitely get their chances to get recharged," Hezkale says.

"Really, how so?"

"Well, the trick with everlasting spells is that when qwitsuls are cast as one of those particular spells, the qwitsuls are instructed to communicate with other qwitsuls independently, calling for whatever unused powerful qwitsuls to take over and mimic the duties of the qwitsuls that need to abandon the everlasting spells to recharge. The qwitsuls' charge isn't what's everlasting when cast as eternal spells; it's what the qwitsuls do that's everlasting."

"So that's how it works." Phoebe rubs her chin with fascination. "Can…everlasting spells be undone or ended?"

"A good amount of them yes, but only by the specific yuets who cast the eternal spells in the first place, while a few other everlasting spells are just straight up permanent and can never be undone no matter how hard everyone tries, including their original casters."

"Which eternal spells can't be undone, even by their original casters?"

"Hmm, the eternal spell cast onto the Vinston and Monston Scepters, which reserves them for royal-blooded Veshael and Xeffizen use. That's a good example."

Phoebe pouts. "Then why would such a spell be cast onto those scepters in the first place?"

"Because that was the only spell that could restrict their usage to only a select few yuets. Everyone was aware of the possible consequences of those scepters having such permanent restrictions with their usage, but the consequences would be far worse if someone as evil as Gaphanagon got a hold of and could work one of those scepters."

Phoebe sighs. "Point taken."

Hezkale motions towards her. "Follow me. I have something else I want to show you."

"This way, Mysty," Phoebe calls, encouraging her kitty to halt scratching her body against the minerals. Heading down one of the paths into the very heart of the garden, Hezkale leads her up to a tremendously high tree with some sort of fruit hanging on its branches. Both the tree and the fruit give off a glow of purple phosphorescence.

"This here is a venny tree. It produces venny berries, a common fruit in Veshael. Would you like to try one?"

Phoebe considers his question for a few seconds and nods her head. Placing Riddy on one of the low hanging limbs, Hezkale leaps up into conveniently arranged branches, which resemble ladder rungs. Jumping from branch to branch, he feels for any ripe venny berries. Phoebe is impressed with his tree-climbing prowess. Finally, coming across a ripe berry, he calls down to her. "Superb! Found a ripe one! Catch!" He tosses the venny berry down. Phoebe keeps a close eye on the purple fruit, watching to see where it's going to land. The berry lands in her hands with an unexpected thud. It's far heavier than she expected. She inspects the fruit carefully—the purple hue of its outer skin doesn't seem to be any one certain colour, instead it appears to glow with countless different shades from the purple spectrum. Although Hezkale called it a berry, there's nothing really berry-like about it. From Phoebe's perspective, it looks more like a pear. Gazing down from the branches above her head, Hezkale gives her a smile of encouragement with his white teeth shining brightly in the darkness. "Go ahead! Try it!"

Phoebe carefully nibbles on the berry. It's so much juicier than she was expecting and the dark purple juice drips off her chin to the ground below. Slowly chewing, she

tries to identify its flavour while at the same time savouring the sweetness. It reminds her of fresh spring strawberries and yet she's quick to identify the slightly more subtle hints of a maple syrup taste in the fleshy fruit. As she takes another bite, she tries to talk with her mouth full.
"Mmm…" is all she manages to get out. She kneels down, holding the fruit out to a curious Mysty. Mysty sniffs it and turns her head away from it snobbishly. "Not to your taste? More for me." Phoebe stands up, happily taking another bite.

Snatching another venny berry for himself, Hezkale jumps down out of the branches. He holds up the fruit and grins at her before taking a big bite. The purple juice drips from his chin and two small drops land on his top quickly spreading into a bright purple stain.

"Oops. Please pardon my messy eating, I just love to eat. Do you like it?"

Phoebe nods.

"I was hoping you would. Of all the fruits in Yuetsion, the venny berry is one of my favourites." He takes another bite. "It's a good thing they're so plentiful. I would eat them for every meal, if more than one per day didn't give me stomach aches."

"Thank you very much for the fruit."

"My pleasure."

Riddy flutters down onto Hezkale's shoulder and stretches his wings to their full length before settling down. Ruffling up his feathers, he glances up at Hezkale with a look of expectancy in his eyes. Phoebe can tell he's trying to mooch some of Hezkale's food. She laughs at his cheekiness. Hezkale lets out a sigh of exasperation before breaking off a piece of fruit. Riddy carefully takes it from Hezkale's fingers and, although he speedily makes the fruit disappear, Phoebe is astonished with how neatly he eats it.

Hezkale watches Riddy, who's fastidiously cleaning his talons. "So, I heard from Hilmina that you seem to really like mincies."

"Mincies?" Phoebe responds with a questioning look.

"Yeah, mincies." Hezkale holds his finger up to Riddy and encourages him to sit on it. He reaches up and scratches the mincy under his chin before continuing to answer Phoebe's question. "Riddy is a mincy."

"Really?"

"Yes. In fact, when we visited your world, I saw some rather interesting looking feathered mincies." He looks thoughtfully at Phoebe. "But I'm guessing you probably call them something else in your world, since you seem to be so unfamiliar with the word mincy."

"Birds...We call them birds."

"Birds huh? That's a catchy name."

"I like the name mincy, too. It…it seems to really fit." She pauses and chuckles a tad, as she scratches Riddy's head a bit, making him whistle contentedly. "On Earth, the closest word to mincy is 'mince'. One of its meanings is to walk daintily."

Hezkale snorts. "That sure doesn't describe Riddy. He likes to make an entrance." He waves her along. "Come on Qelphy, there's still so much to see."

Leaving dust trails in their wake, they travel farther down the pathway and soon find their way blocked by yet another tree. Several large stones can be seen forming a wide protective semi-circle around its trunk. Although this area of the garden doesn't seem to have as much light, Phoebe can clearly make out the shape of the tree, thanks to the miniscule glowing orbs twinkling on its branches. They remind her of fireflies. There appear to be fewer mincies than earlier, but she can still count a large number of them feeding off of the berries. To her astonishment half of the mincies' feathers are emitting beautiful glowing colours from the qwitsuls, just like Hezkale mentioned earlier. Riddy lifts off and joins the rest of the mincies, and Phoebe can just barely make out his dark shape as he settles down on one particular branch.

Hezkale quietly walks up to the tree and sits down on one of the large stones at its base. He slides over and pats the rock, encouraging her to join him. Leaving the pathway, Phoebe walks over and sits down hesitantly on the rock beside him. Curling her tail around her front paws, Mysty sits on the ground at Phoebe's feet and stares up at the mincies perched on the tree.

"What…tree is this?"

"This is a gilgo tree," Hezkale explains. "They're commonly grown throughout Yuetsion, both in gardens and in the wild. The berries they produce are very attractive to mincies. As a matter of fact, they're one of the main food sources for mincies." He makes a sour face. "But yuets can't stand the taste of them."

"There are similar berries on Earth. Some of which are poisonous to humans, but the…birds seem to thoroughly enjoy. There are many different species of birds on Earth. Is it the same with mincies?"

"Oh yes. There are hundreds of thousands of different types of mincies." He points towards where Riddy had landed. "My mincy is a fillynee."

"I really love his purple feathers."

"So do I." He sighs. "I found Riddy when he was still just a baby, walking around on the ground and calling out for his family. He was trying to fly, but he didn't have any flight feathers yet. I picked him up and tried searching for his nest, but was unable to find it. So I decided to look after him myself."

"How do you know Riddy is a he?"

"That's easy. Male fillynee's have purple feathers, whereas the females have green ones so they blend in with their surroundings."

"That makes sense." A wistful appearance leisurely passes across Phoebe's face. "Many of the birds in my world are the same way. The males tend to be more colourful, while the females are drab colours. I think it's because they need to show off when it comes to mating season."

"What's stranger is that between the two of us, we-we are like the mincies," Phoebe says, looking at Hezkale. "I'm the bland-coloured female, while you're practically a rainbow compared to me."

Hezkale laughs. "Oh, Qelphy, where do you get these ideas?"

"My mysterious mind..."

"I suppose so and...now that you've given me the idea, I guess we are pretty similar to the mincies. But we would be the exception to the rule as both male and female yuets of each race have the same body colours. And besides, I don't think you're bland. You have a fine white texture to your skin and very beautiful brown...or red hair."

Phoebe blushes. She feels strangely different in his presence. "Thank you Hezkale. My hair colour is actually brownish-red. The colour is called auburn."

"Auburn, it's a very unique colour."

"Really? You think so?"

"Oh yes, that and your different coloured eyes are more unique than mine, since no yuet has mismatching eyes."

"Seriously?"

"Seriously. Not to mention your clothing is more colourful than mine."

"Thanks, your clothes are neat too." Phoebe gazes up at Riddy, who is nibbling on a gilgo berry. "So are mincies your favourite animals?"

"Oh, yes. I love them very much. I guess that's why I was so disappointed we couldn't stay longer in your world. I would've loved to have been able to see more than just a few birds. Would you say mincies are your favourite animal?"

Phoebe peeks down. Mysty glares up at her jealously. "I...I'd rather not answer that in front of Mysty."

"Who's your friend?"

Phoebe reaches down and lifts Mysty up. Ignoring the kitten's protests, she pats her on the head. "This is Mysty. She's an orange-tabby kitten. She's still a baby and I've only had her a few weeks. Kittens, or cats when they grow up, love to hunt birds and other small creatures. But so far Mysty has been really good with the birds, which makes me happy. Most cats would kill birds, but not her. She seems to be content with just watching them. I'm hoping I can train her to not think of birds as prey."

"Why not get a mincy or bird of your own?"

"Because my mom's allergic to birds, especially their feathers, so I got a kitten instead."

"I see. Is it all right if I touch her?"

"Yes, just let her smell you first. But I must warn you, she rarely takes to strangers."

Hezkale kneels down and extends his hand, palm up, to the orange and white kitten. Mysty sniffs suspiciously before sitting back and giving him the once over. Satisfied he's not going to hurt her, she rubs her head on the backside of his hand.

"Huh, well, she wants you to pet her." Phoebe is quite surprised by Mysty's boldness. Normally she would be hissing by now. During the two weeks she has had Mysty, the kitten has shown a complete distrust of strangers. In fact, she hasn't allowed anyone to touch her except for Phoebe. Even her parents have not had much success gaining her trust. As Hezkale runs his hand along her neck the kitten turns over onto her back, encouraging him to scratch her belly. He's quick to comply and is rewarded with a pleased purr. "She certainly is a noble creature." The kitten jumps up onto the rock between them and nudges

Hezkale's elbow, as if encouraging him to continue petting her. *Maybe Hezkale really is one to trust, if he can win over Mysty so easily, but to be safe I shouldn't give him my full trust. Not yet at least, whether this is all a dream or not.*

"By the way, what do you think of us yuets so far?" Hezkale asks.

"Well…very surprising…" Phoebe says, totally caught off guard. She thinks about the yuets she's met and wonders if there are other yuet races she doesn't know of. "Actually, how many yuet races are there in total?"

"Seven."

"Seven? So, there's more than just…" Phoebe tries to remember the names of the yuet races Cernin taught her about.

"Yes, there are more yuets than Veshaels, Herynes, Kumes and Xeffizens. The remaining three would be Sottenums, Gebawns and Dixidins."

"Really?" Phoebe crosses her legs with interest. "What are they like?"

"Well, they have nothing to do with our quest to take down the Xeffizens, but I can tell you this. Sottenums are undeniably peaceful and highly trustworthy. We may come across a few on our journey. As for the Gebawns and Dixidins, it's best to avoid them if we spot any."

"Why?"

"They're as untrustworthy as the Xeffizens."

"Oh..." Phoebe starts to feel even more nervous, now that she knows there are two other races of corrupt yuets.

"But don't worry. You should be safe as long as you're travelling with us. Besides, the Gebawns and Dixidins aren't as much of a threat as the Xeffizens."

"That's good news...I hope."

Phoebe continues to watch Hezkale play with Mysty, and finds her gaze drawn to something directly behind him. She realizes what she's seeing is his tail swaying back and forth, and its movement is comparable to Mysty's tail just before she's ready to pounce. Captivated, she reaches out and grabs it. Hezkale flinches and grabs his tail out of her hand. Glaring at her, he cradles it protectively in his lap.

"What did I do?" Phoebe asks.

Hezkale sighs. "It's considered extremely rude to grab someone's tail." Phoebe can tell by the way he's holding his tail; he's very displeased with this apparent breach of etiquette.

Ashamed of her irrational mistake, Phoebe blushes and looks away, afraid to face him. "I'm extremely s-s-s-orry, Hezkale. It's just...I'm highly fascinated by your tail. None of the people in my world have tails."

"Ah, I see. That's okay. Now you know for next time."

"Can you please forget that I grabbed your tail?" Phoebe says, focusing back towards Hezkale.

"Certainly."

Relieved, Phoebe sighs. "Thank you. I've watched how you and the others easily walk through the hallways with your tails. But how do you manage to learn to walk with such a long tail?"

Stepping up onto the rock, Hezkale walks back and forth as his tail sways from left to right, in perfect synchronization with each step. He smiles. "We naturally get used to it. I'm sure you've learned many things in your world I wouldn't even know how to do."

Thinking of her highly technological world, Phoebe is inclined to agree with him. "You're probably right."

Phoebe returns her attention to the mincy filled tree. She can just make out Riddy's shape in the darkness of the leafy branches. Hezkale jumps off the rock and quietly returns to sit by her side. A sorrowful expression and slumped shoulders are the only clues as to what's going on.

"Hezkale, what is it? Did I do something wrong?"

"It's not you. I was just thinking about how much Princess Vehilia loved this garden. Whenever she had a free moment to slip away from her royal duties, she would come here. She would spend hours here: smelling the flowers and feeding the mincies and…now that she's gone…nothing seems to be the same anymore."

"I'm very sorry to hear that." Referring back to her possible dream about Princess Vehilia, Phoebe wonders if Hezkale knows any other details about her. "Can I ask what Princess Vehilia was like? I'm…I'm curious to know what my uishanole was like, if you're alright with that?"

"Well…" Hezkale says, tapping his chin, "there's a lot to say about her, but I'll try to summarize her up." He smiles widely. "She was one of the nicest, sweetest, most caring yuet ever. She was always so full of energy. She could be very spoiled at times, not that I really minded. Oh yes, and she highly admired art. She was even an artist herself and her pieces looked very professional, but the funny thing is…" Hezkale chuckled slightly, "she never thought her work was good enough. And she was insanely in love with yether cakes—no one can ever forget that. She was very responsible, more than me, I have to admit. She was extraordinarily compassionate. Her generosity was so grand she wanted to help the poor so much that she literally tossed her expensive jewelry to them."

Phoebe tries not to let her stunned emotion show—he's describing the scene from her dream!

"What's even more impressive is that even though her parents forbid her from tossing the treasures, she didn't give up. She tried to figure out another way to help the poor, like when she convinced her family to contribute clothing, food, shelter and unneeded royal treasures to the poor. My, she was a great influence in the royal meetings. As you can guess, she had a passion for helping others. She was very well-behaved, except when yether cakes came to mind. She normally liked to do what was right…or most of the time, but who's perfect?"

Hezkale smirks.

"She was also the type who liked to be very helpful and useful, even to the point of offering her maids her help too. I always found that pretty funny. Oh! She was also very fond of nature as well. She had her own aviary with tons of mincies that always cheered her up whenever she was in a bad mood and she especially loved her pet golveys.

"Golveys? Wh-what are they?" *Please don't tell me they were those lizards in her bedroom.*

"Oh, they're a popular pet in Yuetsion. They're scaly with aqua and greenish-yellow skin, long tails, forked tongues, claws and sharp teeth. They're bodies are longer than ours. Princess Vehilia had two of them. She named them…"

"Kuzy and Motis," Phoebe and Hezkale say simultaneously.

Hezkale's eyes widen. "How did you know those names? Are…humans like you mind readers?"

"Oh no! I know because…" Phoebe says, trying to come up with a believable excuse. *I can't tell him I dreamed this information—he and the other yuets will think I'm strange. Stranger than they probably already think I am.* "Because…Hilmina already told me about Kuzy and Motis."

Phoebe really hates lying, but she couldn't help it over being too panicked to be truthful.

"Oh, she did?" Hezkale asks.

"Mm-hm."

"Hm, I guess she heard about them through Yorgo or a Veshael."

Phoebe feels a great sense of relief at have avoided a possible commotion. She's still confused about what she saw. If it was a dream, it's uncanny how her dream seems to be unnaturally accurate about this world's past. She trails off deep into thought, feeling apprehensive. *Just what's going on here?! First Cernin talks about things related to the dream I dreamed before I even met him, then the same thing happens with Yorgo and now Hezkale too?! What does all this even mean? Why is this happening?*

"Are you all right Qelphy?"

"I'm fine," Phoebe says, recapturing her focus. "I was just...wondering. How do you kno-know so much detail about Princess Vehilia and her feelings for this garden anyway?"

Hezkale looks at her with pain in his eyes. "Uh...All the Veshaels know about her as much as I do, what she liked and what she did. That's just the way it is on Yuetsion."

"Sounds like yuets must've really looked up to her."

"Many of them, yes. Most of them looked at her as an extraordinary hero," Hezkale says, "while others would've been respectful out of duty and a few were downright jealous."

Phoebe laughs. "Do you think there are any yuets who didn't like or even hate her?"

"That would be the Xeffizens," Hezkale says, brusquely.

"Oh...sorry I asked." Phoebe feels guilty and embarrassed for asking.

"No, it's fine for you to ask. I'm sorry for reacting so bluntly," Hezkale says, easing up. "The Xeffizens really took too much from us Veshaels, so we'd rather not be reminded about them."

"I'm very sorry this had to happen to all of you. I'll try my best to not ask you about them anymore."

"Thank you Qelphy, you're very kind, but it's actually very good for you to ask questions about them. You need to know what they're like, the perils they can create and how you should face them. Feel free to ask me or the others if you need to know anything."

"Okay, thank you."

Hezkale shrugs his shoulders as if to rid himself of his gloomy mood. He whistles for Riddy. The mincy wings his way back from the tree and lands on Hezkale's shoulder. He strokes his wild pet. "Say, not that I mean to be rude, but ever since I've met you, I've noticed you kind of talk and act…differently."

"Oh, well…yes, I do." Phoebe says uncomfortably.

"Does everyone in your world talk and act the way you do?"

"No. Most people talk fine like you. It's…how I function."

"Why is that?"

"It…" Phoebe looks away shyly and gloomily. *It's my autism that makes me the way I am.* "It's too complex to explain. I'm just…different and…I became this way when I-I-I was a toddler."

"Hmm, I see." Hezkale rubs his chin, studying her.

Phoebe folds her hands behind her and stares at her feet. "Do you…have a problem with the way I am?"

"Of course not!"

She glances at him, feeling a sense of optimism grow.

"You mean…you won't judge me?" Phoebe asks, unfolding her palms.

"I don't have reason to," Hezkale says, shrugging his shoulder.

"And you won't bully me?" Phoebe's eyebrows frown for a second whenever she says or hears the word 'bully'.

"I'm not that kind of yuet," Hezkale says.

"… Really?"

"Really."

"But why?" Phoebe asks.

Hezkale smiles, as he exhales through his nose with some laughter. "I'd never want to mistreat you. That's why."

Phoebe's body and mind loosen up. In fact, she realizes she's presently staring straight into his eyes, which is very rare for her. Generally her autism makes her too shy to look any stranger in the eye, but looking directly into his eyes she finds the colouration gorgeous, especially the silky texture of his purple irises.

"Thank…thank you very much," Phoebe says.

"You're very welcome, Qelphy."

Maybe…my time in this world or dream won't be too bad with Hezkale by my side.

"Anyway, it's getting late. We better head off to bed. Tomorrow is going to be a big day. I'll show you back to your room if that's okay." He turns to lead the way back through the garden. Although Phoebe is anxious to learn more about her uishanole, she realizes getting some sleep is probably the best option to do at the moment.

"Hezkale, I just have one more question."

He turns around with a quizzical expression on his face. "Oh?"

"How old are you?"

"I'm thirteen. Why?"

Delighted her suspicions have been confirmed, she smiles at him. "Me too!"

Hezkale laughs. "I had a feeling you were close to my age, since you look no older than Princess Vehilia." And with that he starts heading back to her chambers. While she follows his swishing tail, it occurs to her: *That's probably the longest conversation I've ever had with anyone, let alone someone my own age.*

Chapter 9

    While Mysty purrs contentedly on the pillow beside her, Phoebe tosses and turns for an hour in her bed, until she gets up in defeat and starts treading restlessly around the perimeter of the bedroom. The reason behind her sleeplessness isn't the glow of her amethyst necklace, since its glow is faint and the blankets cover it or the qwitsuls' constant radiance with them being only bright enough to be dim night lights. It's all her thoughts about uishanoles and fighting Xeffizens combined with the probability of her never returning home again, leaving her wakeful. Pacing around the room for several minutes, she finally sits at the desk tucked against one wall. Turning on one of the crystal lamps, she stares at herself in the mirror.

    "What am I going to do? How am I ever going to get myself through this or out of this?" Phoebe rubs her eyes under her glasses in frustration. "I can't just run away in this alien world. That will only make my situation worse." She focusses back on her reflection, getting surprised. The girl's resolute expression eyeing back at her is the last entity she would've expected to see. Her autism tends to make her view life more desirably, making her determination for accomplishing her goals strong enough to never give up until her objectives are fulfilled, but her willpower habitually hasn't been this extreme until now. Somehow, this entire experience is altering her spirit. "I guess...I only have one option, dream or not. I need to stop trying to run away and actually agree to help these yuets destroy the Monston Scepter. If that's the only way I can get home, then that's exactly what I'm going to do.

However, the hardest thing about all this is…not knowing what will happen. What terrifies me the most about all this is…having no idea what the wicked yuets and fearsome creatures of this world are capable of or what other dangers lie ahead. Hopefully Hezkale and the others will tell me what I can expect to experience. Well, the most important thing right now is…to do whatever it takes for me and Mysty to get home. I…" She blinks with realization. "To be with my parents again, I have to become The Bright and Shining Flower of Hope of this world."

She gazes down at her necklace's gemstones, rubbing her fingers gently across their polished surfaces. Aside from Mysty, her jewelry is the one connection to her family.

"Mom…Dad…I promise I will make it back home to you. No matter what happens, we will see each other again."

Chapter 10

Phoebe winces as light penetrates her tightly closed eyelids, waking her with a start. Only moments before, she'd been in bed, visualizing a leafy canopy, listening to enchanting birdsongs, while the maple trees swayed overhead. Now everything's blurry, almost as if someone's covered her eyes in spider silk. The floor beneath her feels cool, but inside her head there's a fiery chaos. Ignoring the painful pulsating of her headache, she attempts to sit up. A wave of nausea so intense she almost blacks out threatens to prevent any further attempts to get up off the glassy stone floor. After several more aborted attempts to stand up, the throbbing in her head subsides enough for her to manage it.

It takes several seconds for her eyes to adjust—then she realizes where she is. The mirror-filled labyrinth is spread out before her, but this particular area feels different somehow. She's in the middle of a cylinder-like room with twelve hallways that intersect in the centre and lead off in various directions. Shimmering curtains of qwitsuls dance everywhere, especially at the entrance of each hallway, encouraging Phoebe to explore. Hundreds of mirrors and stained glass windows cover every wall.

I'm back in the mirrored chambers again! Am I dreaming the same dream all over again? Wait...If I am, then why does it feel so different? These are most definitely qwitsuls flowing everywhere, so I must still be in Yuetsion. Could it be possible that I'm transporting to different areas whenever I sleep? And...for some odd reason...I'm starting to get this...submerging feeling...like...I'm underground somewhere. Could this maybe be what Yuetsion is like deep underground?

Phoebe gazes nervously around the room.

Since I'm back here, does this mean I'll come across that monster again?!

An echoing causes her to hesitate. She waits for the inevitable to happen. Nothing.

I guess it's not here or...at least not right now...

Stepping forward, her foot nudges against a firm object. Drawing her attention downwards: the Vinston Scepter gleams luminously on the floor! Picking it up, she's surprised by how comfortable its touch has become despite its appearance. As much as she wonders where it keeps coming from, she doesn't feel it's worth questioning knowing this labyrinth is as bizarre as Wonderland. *So this is the Vinston Scepter.* Aiming it in a random direction, she's disappointed when nothing happens. Shaking it seems to yield the same result. *Right, I need to say the right incantation in order for something to happen.*

"Abracadabra...! Hocus pocus...!"

Still nothing.

I guess the spell casting works differently. Cernin did say I'd be taught some spells, but I wonder how effective they'll be if I cast them using this scepter. Then again, I hope the scepter doesn't work for me, so they'll have to let me go back home. She glances around. *I just hope I don't come across that monster again.*

She's gazing down the hallways when something firm grips her left hand's ring finger. When she peeks down she discovers she's wearing the same ring Hezkale had loaned her earlier.

I'm wearing Hezkale's ring?! Maybe I am teleporting after all!

Phoebe frowns.

Though, then again, anyone can dream about anything, even if the dream feels realistic...

Phoebe sighs, and lets her hand drop. *Which way should I go?* She stares down at the scepter, hoping it will guide her, but once again it does nothing. Taking her chances, Phoebe turns left, pacing slowly across the floor toward one of the hallways while keeping a close and wary eye on her surroundings. Holding the scepter firmly, she waits to see what will happen. If something were to happen, the firmness of the scepter could easily double as a makeshift weapon.

An abrupt whistle causes her to jump. Looking down at the scepter, she sees the mincy statue has come to life again. It stretches its wings and dances impatiently on top of the blue orb. "You're alive again!" Phoebe yells. The mincy lifts off from the scepter and makes a lazy loop of the room before flying towards one particular hallway. Running after it, Phoebe finds it almost impossible to keep up. "Hey wait! Wait for me!"

The mincy lands near the entrance and waits for her. After reaching the hallway, Phoebe puts her hands on her knees in an attempt to catch her breath. Before she's able to take more than a few gasps of air, it flies off down the aisle. Phoebe has no choice but to follow.

If it's that desperate to show me something, the least it could do is give me a chance to catch my breath.

With one last glance back, the mincy disappears into a passage. Phoebe can see a flight of stairs seeming to cross a bottomless chasm with the mincy waiting at the other side. Phoebe peers down before nervously beginning her descent. *Hopefully I won't fall.* She watches her footing carefully, pushing any thought of falling from her mind. Once she reaches the other side, sighing with relief, she turns her attention to the environment. She's in a cavernous area linked to two hallways, each one with statues of Veshaels and Herynes wielding scepters, their expressions of contempt turned downwards towards her. *Statues of yuets! This must be a part of Yuetsion after all!* The mincy waves its wing as it whistles her over. She ignores the statues and runs up to the mincy.

The glow from one particular mirror on the wall snags her attention. She looks back down at the mincy, which gazes up at Phoebe with glowing blue eyes. It cocks its head to the left, signaling for her to look into the mirror. Its brightness causes her to squint before her eyesight dims enough so she can see her reflection. She's not surprised to see the image of Princess Vehilia. *Alright, I know she's Princess Vehilia, I know she's my uishanole and I know that I'm holding the Vinston Scepter, but I still don't understand what this all means.* Princess Vehilia gently waves Phoebe forwards.

"Y-you want me…to follow you?" Phoebe asks.

The princess nods her head and vanishes.

"Wait," Phoebe calls, "Come back!"

The mincy soars straight into the mirror and vanishes as well. Phoebe cautiously reaches a hand out towards the mirror and tenses, remembering the sensation of getting sucked in. She's absorbed into the mirror so rapidly she doesn't even have time to scream. Her eyelids open, and all around her she can see qwitsuls covering everything. She's on a diamond-shaped brick street with red crystal lamps and clouded structures surrounding her. Like the holograms in her first labyrinth visit, all the yuets have qwitsuls concealing their identities. As she stands there, some of them swish right through her.

Wait a minute—it's bright out, so how come I can see the qwitsuls?

Phoebe spots Princess Vehilia in a black dress and black gloves, with a teal-coloured crystal crown. She looks approximately nine years old, but more poised than Phoebe was at that age. She's surrounded by twenty towering yuets, bodyguards of some sort, as she strolls down the street. Passersby move aside, giving the royal procession space, and immediately bow. The princess gives them courteous waves and flashes a friendly smile.

Then it comes: a rumbling in the distance. The crowds begin to panic. *A stampede?* The yuets flee into nearby buildings and duck into shelters, emptying the streets. Princess Vehilia's guards immediately hoist her off the ground and carry her to the nearest building, but the doorway is crammed with bodies. The yuets scream and press, trying to get inside, but many are left trapped in the streets. Phoebe knows she can't be affected by what's happening but feels scared regardless. She focuses back on the princess, who's nearing a packed doorway—but she seems to be resisting.

"Come, your highness!" a male guard shouts. "Get inside for your own safety!"

"Not until everyone else is safe!" Princess Vehilia demands.

"There's no more room in the building," shouts another guard, this one female. "We can only protect a handful of them!"

"Then let's blast a few of the creatures and try to scare the herd away!" the male guard yells. "That'll sort them out."

"You are not to kill any animals, I command you!" the princess shouts.

"Then what? What can we do?"

In the press of the fleeing yuets, surrounded by shouts and screams, Princess Vehilia reaches into the folds of her clothes and produces a scepter with a brown mast, its crystal sphere turquoise. Her guards lower her to the ground and she dashes forward, weaving between the other yuets, and aims the scepter at the street. Phoebe's eyes widen as a qwitsul ray jets from the scepter's crystal, striking the brickwork and ricocheting into a massively curved twenty-foot crystal peak of multiple colours. The jagged mineral formation screeches and tinkles, reaching over the nearby rooftops. *There's nothing like that on Earth.*

"Do exactly what I did throughout the rest of town!" Vehilia says, handing the scepter back to one of her guards. "Everyone will be able to climb up the crystals to the rooftops! Quick, spread out and get to work!"

Her bodyguards sprint in different directions while one remains by her side, following as she clambers up to the crystal peak she created. They begin using its spikes, ledges and cracks to climb until they reach the flat roof of the nearest structure, while the rest of the yuets follow their example. Phoebe can hear the tinkling crash of other peaks forming around town, and the shouts as other yuets ascend out of danger. It's just as they're reaching safety that the thundering—which Phoebe had almost forgotten until that moment—becomes deafening. She turns to see unusual-looking animals that seem better suited for the ocean. They have green scaly, fish-like exteriors and they're the size of a hippo with eight sprinting, white-clawed legs. Their toothless mouths gape open while their purple eyes bulge out balloon-like. As they approach, she covers her ears, disgusted by their wailing.

The creatures crash through lampposts, shatter crystals, dent the brickwork streets and smash through the buildings' lower walls. One rushes right through Phoebe and her mincy, which startles her for a moment before she remembers they can't hurt her. The stampede continues for a few minutes, the ground shaking, but eventually they pass. Phoebe glances up to see yuets tentatively returning to the street.

"Let's hear it for our princess!" shouts one yuet from the rooftops. "Let's hear it for Princess Vehilia!"

Applause breaks out as Vehilia appears at the edge of the rooftop, gazing down at the street. She bows gracefully and places her fists on her hips, heroine-like. Phoebe stares up at her. *Wow, she really is something. She defends herself from murder, now she puts the life of her citizens before her own and manages to save everyone who couldn't get into the buildings...and at such a young age too!*

The mincy squawks, summoning the qwitsuls, and their location transforms into a room with four long, interconnected stone tables. They're elaborately carved. It doesn't take her long to spot Vehilia again, who's wearing a thin green dress and looking Phoebe's age. She's listening as men plead with her.

"We've successfully contributed shelter, clothing and plenty of food for the poor thanks to your great ideas, your majesty," says one of the yuets. "Your citizens are quite grateful."

"It was my pleasure to help," Vehilia says, "and my duty."

"I wonder—do you have any other ideas you might share with us?"

Vehilia smiles, folding her white-gloved hands on the table. "Oh, yes," she says. "I've been doing some thinking and I've thought about giving away the treasures we no longer need. I have plenty of trinkets I'm no longer interested in, and they aren't of any historical importance."

"That's quite generous," says the yuet. "That sounds like a great idea."

A yuet woman steps in. "I've received word that the Gebawns are even more out of control with their thievery. They've been stealing from rich and poor alike. I can't help but feel that giving away our treasures to the poor will only encourage the Gebawns. If you want my advice, I believe it would be best to keep the treasure within castle walls."

Je-bons? Didn't Hezkale mention them once?

"But giving the poor our unneeded treasures would be a useful way of giving them the funds to stay alive, at least for a time," Princess Vehilia says. "Isn't that more important?"

"The Gebawns aren't going to stop stealing unless we start fighting back!" someone shouts. "We need to take the fight to them!"

"We can't create another war!" shouts another. "We've already got one to deal with!"

"Then we must convince the Gebawns to change their ways," Vehilia says. "That's the only option."

"It's not that simple!"

"No, but I believe that no matter how troublesome yuets may be, they can still be redeemed if they're given the opportunity to change. Yes, they steal—but they're not as bad as a couple other races we've been confronted with."

"So how should we approach this?"

Vehilia thinks for a moment. "We must find a compromise with the Gebawn monarch. We must convince them to change their nation's ways. If I can reason with them, perhaps we can convince them that an end to thievery will benefit all of us. And together we can reap the rewards."

"Then it's settled, you'll meet with the monarch?" one yuet asks. "Will it be you that personally negotiates with the monarch?"

Vehilia nods, and though they begin to applaud, she holds up her hand. Phoebe can't help but be amazed. *I'd love to have a friend as strong and kind as her. One who won't mind my autism and will like me as I am. Or better yet: a boyfriend!* The clapping stops and everyone leans closer to hear what the princess will say next.

"We haven't reached the time of applause yet," she says. "There's still work to be done." And just as she speaks those words, the mincy sings again, this time transporting Phoebe to a garden similar to the one she toured with Hezkale and Hilmina, but on a grander scale. The mincy flies back onto the Vinston Scepter and freezes in place in its original pose. Phoebe glances about and sees a young Veshael boy, about five years old, sitting on a rock next to a pond. He's wearing a dark blue shirt with green fractal designs stitched into it and plain black pants. He gazes down at his reflection in the water, looking morose. As she watches, a paper mincy glides into a nearby maple-like tree with pink branches and blue leaves.

Where did that come from?

She hears rustling in the nearby shrubs. A young Princess Vehilia, same age as the boy, jogs up to the tree with the hem of her pink dress clutched in one hand.

"My mincy!" she says.

The boy notices her and gasps, bowing instantly.

"You don't have to do that," she says. "It's okay, stand up."

"But…you're Princess Vehilia."

"Then I order you not to do that," she says authoritatively. She squints back up at her toy in irritation. "Could you please get my toy…if you can?"

The boy looks up at the mincy in the tree. "Okay."

The boy effortlessly climbs the tree and whacks the toy down with his tail. Princess Vehilia catches it joyfully and he slides down the tree trunk.

"Thank you very much!" she says.

"It wasn't even that high," he says, sinking back down on the rock. Phoebe can see his rippling reflection in the pond, and he looks depressed.

"What's wrong?"

"I've…just lost my family and…I'm all alone now."

"Oh…I'm very sorry to hear that. What happened to them?"

The boy sighs, looking upwards. "My house was swallowed up by a giant sinkhole…while my mother and father were still inside—and they weren't the only ones. Our neighbours, families all around us…"

"That's terrible! I can't believe it. The whole town fell in?"

"Most of it, yes." The boy grips his legs and his head slouches down. "Now…I have nothing. Nothing." Tears leak from his eyes, but he tries his best to hide them. Phoebe feels just as bad for the boy as Vehilia.

I can't imagine going through something like that.

"I'm so sorry." Princess Vehilia thinks for a bit and smiles holding out her toy mincy to him. "Would you like to play with me?"

Lifting his head, his watery eyes look at her in surprise. "Really? Do you mean it?"

"Actually, I meant…would you like to be my friend?"

Overcome by this unexpected request, the boy's face transforms. "Ye…Yes…I'd love to," the boy says, brushing his tears aside. He joyfully leaps off the stone. "My name is Hezkale."

Phoebe's stunned. *Hezkale?!* Observing him closer, she can make out the resemblance. *That little boy is Hezkale!* But just as she's figured that out the qwitsuls begin to flow again, whirlwind-like, pulling her back into the mirrored labyrinth.

The images of Princess Vehilia, Hezkale and the garden begin to dissolve as the qwitsuls flow into the area like a whirlwind. Once the qwitsuls cease, Phoebe discovers she's back in the mirrored labyrinth.

"**Phoebe…Phoebe…Phoebe…**," echoes a familiar monstrous voice.

Growing fearful, Phoebe feels her blood thickening, as a sense of pure evil lurks closely. She scans the nearby hallways until she spots its malicious eyes peering back at her, and with that, she flees in the opposite direction.

I don't know how much more of this I can take! When is it going to end?!

Phoebe sprints toward the double doors at the end of the hall. A small sliver of light appears as one of them cracks open with just enough room for her to squeeze through. She gasps, as she comes across a gargantuan, spacious hall…which is completely upside down! The ground, the flipped Kume statues, everything!

"What's happening?!" Phoebe cries.

"**I'm coming for you Phoebe…**," the monster calls.

Phoebe begins to cry. *What, do I jump?! If I jump from this height, I could die!* She wipes her tears to stop them blurring her eyes and notes her surroundings. A small ledge sticking out of the wall connected to the doorway seems to be her only means of escape. *This is going to be dangerous, but the monster is coming!* She tosses the Vinston Scepter onto the ledge on the other side of the door. Cautiously, she clings onto the door and dangles. She swings herself to the ledge and hastily steps onto it, grabbing hold of the mirrors' frames with one hand, and picks up the Vinston Scepter with her free hand. Her entire body is shaking and she's gasping for breath. Using the mirrors as finger holds, she starts creeping slowly along the wall of mirrors until she finds herself entangled. She looks at the sticky string wrapped around her and discovers she's climbed right into a massive spider web. She screams, disgusted. Peeking over her shoulder, she's shocked to find there are giant spider webs all over the area.

Where did all this come from?!

A thought pops into her mind.

Wait, the last time I was here, the monster took on the form of a giant wolf/dog creature that was part man and I'm afraid of dogs. Does this mean the monster is taking on a different form that I'm afraid of? She glances back at the silken strands. She can hear eerie tapping sounds and glass shatters in the distance. She peers down the hall and sees the shadowy monster appear again, but this time he looks as if he's half man and half spider! He has eight piercing legs, long fingers with sharp claws constantly wiggling as he walks and a long lizard tail, instead of a spider's round behind. The only similarity between this monster's form and his last form is the way his two eyeballs on his bald head look. He stares straight at her and bares his wickedly sharp teeth.

"Found you, Phoebe."

Phoebe screams and moves across the wall with as much agility as she can muster. The monster walks up the wall and upside down onto the ceiling. He spits large webs onto the walls, and the sight immediately leaves her feeling nauseous. She fights through the webs as the monster gets closer, but then Phoebe turns and aims the glowing scepter at him.

"I have the Vinston Scepter! And I'll…I'll blast-blast you with it, if you come any cl-closer!" Phoebe says, shouting at the top of her lungs.

The monster grins down at his prey. **"Go ahead. You know nothing about qwitsul spell casting."**

Phoebe's anger slowly dissolves into hopelessness. The monster swipes his massive claws and smacks them against the wall, smashing the mirrors. The tremors cause Phoebe to lose her fragile grip on the mirrors. She screams as she falls and lands on one of the giant spider webs below. Struggling to get out of the web, she finds the strings have adhered to her clothing and are too strong for her to break loose from. The monster laughs hideously as it creeps down the wall towards her. Phoebe shakes her body around, trying to loosen herself from the web, but unfortunately, it makes no difference.

"Struggle all you want, you'll never escape me. Now don't worry, I'll go easy on you…by not chewing before I swallow."

She stares at the monster. Her fear is so intense she can't even gulp. All she can do is cry.

The Vinston Scepter begins glowing brighter in her hands. "**No!**" The monster shouts. Phoebe shrieks, as he furiously attempts snatching her with his boney hand. As his claws inch closer, the scepter rapidly brightens up the expanse of the location, until Phoebe can observe nothing but whiteness. Everything instantaneously dissolves away.

Chapter 11

Phoebe opens her eyes. The dark visions of her latest encounter with the spider creature slowly fade away. She's back in her Yuetsion bedroom. Mysty slumbers at her waist, so she gently strokes her head while she calms down. Her forehead is drenched in sweat. *If I sweat anymore I could fill my own waterbed. I wonder what time it is.* Often she has difficulty falling back to sleep after waking up in the middle of the night. Her inability to do so has always frustrated her. She has always been left feeling supremely groggy and, unlike the adults in her life, she's not allowed to drink the magical elixir known as coffee.

But in this case, she's relieved at her inability to get back to sleep. At least she won't have to face the monster again. *What's up with that monster and its eyes?!* Phoebe sits up gently so as not to wake Mysty and contemplates the mirrored labyrinth. *Let's see, when I fell asleep, I woke up in the mirrored labyrinth and when that bright flash of light blinded me, I woke back up in Yuetsion and this happened twice. So...Ugh! I still don't have any useful information to find out whether Yuetsion or the mirrored place is a dream or not!*

The rumbling of thunder outside makes Phoebe jump. She looks over at the nearest window and watches the storm through a small gap in the curtains. The lightning streaks across the sky with each bolt leaving the impression of a camera flash. She knows it's going to bother her all night. Getting out of bed, she walks over to the window, pulls open the curtains and peers out. Phoebe finds herself wanting to stare out the window all night, but a creaking noise catches her attention. Then a shadow appears on the other side of the glass, a dark figure. Lightning flashes behind him as he bares his teeth. Phoebe screams and pulls the curtain closed just before it shatters inward. She snags a startled Mysty and scrambles under the bed to hide.

Two large grey bare feet with long black sharp claws land on the ground. The creature steps in between the glass shards, making way for another pair of monstrous feet to follow.

"Wha ya lookin fer?" asks a man's voice.

"I thought I saw someone in here," grunts the other man's voice. "She looked like a little girl. She must've run away."

To Phoebe, their voices sound very deep with a couple grunts, yet quite loud, even though they sound like they're talking in normal tones. Despite the one's overly slangy speech, Phoebe can comprehend what he's saying. The man's voice laughs.

"Is jus like ya ta scare the females way," the man's voice says.

"Ah, shut it you. I scared her away on purpose to save us the hassle of dragging an obnoxious little brat around the whole time. By the way, do you happen to know where Captain Wazure is?"

Captain Way-zure? Who's that?

"He should be in the middle of the tower by now. Les locate 'em, before we get blamed fer slackin off."

Mysty hisses at the intruders and Phoebe covers her mouth. *Please stay quiet for our life's sake Mysty!*

"Did you hear something?"

Oh no! They're going to find me! What will they do to me?!

"Ah, probably nothin important."

She watches their feet as they approach the door and starts to make out more of their bodies' appearance. It's hard to tell from this distance—even the qwitsuls aren't enough to provide a sharp view of them—but she can definitely see they're twice the height of an average man, or maybe even a little more, like about fourteen feet high! Their hulking frames dwarf the bedroom. She watches them open the door and crouch to get through it. *Who are they?! What are they?! Are they giants?! Are they giant yuets?! Why are they here?!*

Phoebe doesn't dare come out from under her bed, so she waits underneath it with Mysty for about twenty minutes. She refuses to wipe away any of her tears because she's too terrified to take her eyes off the door. To her surprise, Cernin sprints7u unexpectedly into her room. This time he's dressed more formally, wearing a long sleeved dark blue tuxedo, black khakis with a hole for his tail, a belt holding a big strange looking gun and a brown hand held bag wrapped over his shoulder. She can see he's frightened.

"Qelphy?!" Cernin whispers. "Qelphy?! Qelphy?! Are you here?! Where are you?!"

Phoebe wants to be saved, but her body won't cooperate and she finds herself too petrified to move or call out. She's also trying to decide if she's safer by remaining hidden from the giants under the bed alone or scurrying around the building with Cernin with the risk of coming across the hulks. She watches Cernin's feet run up to her bed and hears him searching through the sheets.

"Oh no...No! No! Qelphy!"

Phoebe watches him dash out of her room, disappearing down one of the hallways. She bangs her head against the ground in frustration, hating herself for losing what may have been her only chance of rescue and the better option for survival. *Why did my fear have to keep me from doing anything to get Cernin's attention?! Why?!* Phoebe waits for thirty more minutes under the bed. She hasn't seen anyone pass by her door for quite a while. *Should I go out now…? Is it safe…? I haven't seen anyone lately. Maybe…I just…might.* She gulps nervously, crawling out from under the bed, while holding onto Mysty. She stands up unsteadily, trying her best to keep her sleepy legs balanced and hurriedly walks to the door. Tucking Mysty into her skirt pocket to avoid losing her, she carefully pokes her head out of the doorway. A quick peek to her left and right tells her no one is there.

Phoebe silently roams down the halls, peering into rooms as she passes by, horrified by the destruction she sees. The beautiful crystal lamps and statuary lie in shattered pieces on the floor, but the crystal shards still shimmer in the dim light. Doors leading to many of the rooms have been torn apart and many dangle haphazardly from their hinges. Phoebe cautiously treads her way through the devastation carefully avoiding the broken fragments of crystal on the floor. All of this damage couldn't possibly be the work of just those two giant yuets alone. The tension in the air is so intense Mysty emits a low growl from her place in Phoebe's pocket. She definitely doesn't trust the appearances of their surroundings.

"Right you are Mysty," Phoebe whispers.

Phoebe glances into another torn up room and covers her mouth with her hand to prevent a scream of anger from escaping. The features are instantly recognizable. It's the lab where she had been taken to meet Cernin. Fragments of glass from test tubes, beakers and windows litter the floor. The sparkling shards create the illusion of sheets of ice. Chemicals stain the floor and walls and Phoebe can see evidence of areas where some of the stronger chemicals have melted through the floor. She spots Cernin's scepter, illuminating redness, lying on the ground near the lab's entrance. *It's Cernin's scepter!* Phoebe remembers all the magnificent qwitsul magic it had displayed earlier. *I wonder if I should use it for protection, but I don't even know any of the spells.* Phoebe examines the damage again. These monstrous giants must be very dangerous indeed. *Hmm...Then again, it's better than nothing. It even looks solid enough to smack it hard against those giant yuets after all.* Sidestepping the broken glass, she reaches warily for the scepter and rubs her fingers along its length. It doesn't seem to have suffered any damage. The scepter's location near the doors has protected it from the chemicals which continue to eat through the floor. She picks it up and to her astonishment it's not as heavy as it looks. Mysty anxiously meows and Phoebe holds her paw.

"Don't worry," Phoebe whispers. "I'm sure we'll be fine…"

Phoebe carefully makes her way down the passage for what seems to be quite a long period of time. The hall makes a quick turn to the right and she uncontrollably freezes in fear. There are five of those giant yuets in the hall! The one facing her spots her and gestures to his companions. They all turn to look in her direction. In the crystalline light of the wall lamps, Phoebe can plainly see what their appearances are. Their hairless bodies' predominant skin colour is ash gray slashed with black stripes and the bright silver colours of their palms, neck's fronts, bellies and undersides of their long lizard-like tails contrast against the rest of their skin. Their faces seem horizontally elongated and they don't have noses, just two nose holes, giving them a raptor-like appearance. Compared to Phoebe's eyes, their double-sized eyes contain red sclera, yellow irises and black skin on and around their eyelids extending two inches outwards. They have huge sharp black teeth and lengthy thick black claws on their fingers and toes. Held together by brown belts, black loin cloths wrap around their waists and tails. Strapped to their belts are sword-sized daggers, colossal swords and miniature sack-sized pockets. One is overweight, one is chubby, one is skinny, one is very muscular and the last one has a normal-sized looking body, but with crooked teeth. They're way scarier looking than the bullies from her school and their creepy smiles make her feel like prey.

"You lost little child?" the muscular one asks.

Speechless, Phoebe begins to back away, but she stiffens with a gasp, as they hastily surround her. She gazes up into five pairs of threatening eyes.

"Careful! She has a scepter," the chubby yuet says.

"She's just a child. How harmful can she be?" the overweight yuet says.

"Hey...I think I know her," the skinny yuet says, pointing down at her with a crooked smile. "Yes I do! You're the girl from that bedroom, aren't you?"

"I guess we missed one," the yuet with the crooked teeth says.

"Well, she's ours now," the chubby yuet says. He reaches for her but for some reason he hesitates. "Say, she smells diffrent."

"What do you mean different?"

"She...," the chubby man says, sniffing a little more. "Smell like nothin I ever smelled before." They all begin to sniff the air, while Phoebe stares up at them uneasily. *Why are they smelling me?! Is it the odour from the scepter they smell?!*

"You're right," the muscular yuet says. "She does smell odd. Hand me the crystal."

The muscular yuet is handed a bright glowing green crystal by the yuet with the crooked teeth from his belt pocket. He kneels down and holds it up to Phoebe's face, forcing her to lean away. They see her face and instantaneously gasp, backing away from her in shock. The muscular man drops the crystal and shakily points at Phoebe.

"Impossible!" the muscular man says. "You-you're Princess Vehilia! You should be dead!"

Despite how frightened she is, she realizes they've backed far enough away for her to attempt an escape. Knowing she can't let her fear make her falter now, she takes advantage of the situation and starts to run as fast as she can.

"Hold it!" says the overweight yuet. He tries blocking Phoebe, but she hastily sprints right through his long legs without needing to crouch, whacking his fat tail out of her way with the scepter.

"Get her!" the muscular yuet shouts.

The yuets quickly charge down the passageways after her. Phoebe rushes with all her strength. She's careful to make sure Mysty won't fall out of her pocket.

"Ya canna outrun us!" hollers the chubby yuet.

As she continues her headlong flight, it soon becomes apparent the yuets are right behind her. She spots a wooden table leaning against the wall up ahead. Rushing past it, she pulls it down in a single fluid motion behind her, effectively blocking the hallway. Her pursuers are so intent on catching her they don't notice the table in time and the first one to reach the obstacle trips over it and falls to the ground. His companions topple right onto him.

"You won't get away!" the skinny yuet shouts, as they struggle to get up.

Without checking behind, Phoebe sprints into the hallway on her left and crashes into a leg.

"What the?!" an enormous yuet shouts, at least sixteen feet tall. He turns and glares down at Phoebe, who's gaping up at him. He has a large round belly bigger than Yorgo's, monstrous muscles, a vast thick chin, a long thick lizard-like tail and a scratched up, blind left eye. He's got a belt wrapped around his waist with a double-sized sword, a dagger and a hatchet.

"What have we got here?" the massive yuet says, kneeling down in front of her. The other five yuets Phoebe encountered earlier rush into the hall. Their surprised eyes lock onto the large yuet and they hold their fists to their chests.

"Captain Wazure sir!"

This is Captain Wazure?! He's the one causing all this?!

"Captain Wazure," the skinny yuet says. "That girl...she's Princess Vehilia."

"HAH!" laughs Wazure. "Don't make me laugh."

Wazure grabs Phoebe's arm tightly, making her cringe. His tight grip makes her extremely uncomfortable.

"Ah, stop resisting little girl and let me see your face, if you want us to go easy on you," Wazure says. He lifts Phoebe high into the air, holding her arm. She tries kicking her legs wildly, but he's holding her too far away. Mysty hisses as he raises her up to the crystal light. He stares intensely into Phoebe's eyes, becoming stunned. "Vehilia…" He studies her body shape and colours and sniffs her scent to figure out what kind of yuet she is. "No…She's not even a yuet. She would have to be…the uishanole…"

Captain Wazure's deduction shocks the other yuet goliaths.

"Whas she doin ere?" asks the crooked toothed yuet.

"Don't you remember why we came here in the first place?!" Wazure shouts. "Our king's spies were growing increasingly suspicious of the yuets who were visiting Hiljin Tower in great numbers a little too often. He forced some of this group's captured yuets to reveal what these traitors have been up to, and imagine his surprise when he discovered that the plan was to take a royal blooded Veshael's uishanole to wield the Vinston Scepter. And here she is…"

"What should we do with her?"

"We'd normally do what the king demands, but he never gave us any instructions about dealing with an uishanole." Wazure uses his empty hand to reach for one of the swords attached to his belt. "But I know what's best for our race and that's to kill her before she has the chance to wield the Vinston Scepter." He slips it out of his belt and points it at Phoebe. He chuckles as she panics, struggling to free herself from his grip. "You certainly are a panicky little one. Don't worry; your death will be nice and quick. In fact, you won't even feel a thing."

"Help!" Phoebe screams. *He's going to kill me!*

Abruptly, Hezkale charges into the hall gripping the two swords from his bedroom. He swipes the sword at Wazure's leg, cutting it badly. Violet blood spills out and Wazure yells out in pain as he drops Phoebe. She's sickened by the violence, and she stares at the blood on the ground. It looks like grape juice. She checks on Mysty in her pocket quickly, as other oversized yuets flood into the room and draw their swords.

Riddy swiftly soars into the area. He flies up into the giant yuets' faces flapping his wings, pecking at them and scratching their faces with his claws to distract them. Hezkale quickly slips one of his swords into the black belt around his waist and grabs Phoebe's hand. They dash down one of the hallways, and though Phoebe feels really uncomfortable with him grabbing her hand, in this case she'll make an exception. Riddy soars beside them.

"Don't let them get away!" Wazure roars.

"Don't worry!" Hezkale says. "I know how we can lose them! There's a way out of this area! Just try to keep up with me!"

I can keep up with you, just please keep leading! Unfortunately, two more of the yuets come into view from an intersecting hall ahead of them. They rapidly move into the entrance to block their path. Phoebe's heart drops as she turns to look back, sighting they're still being pursued from behind too. "We're trapped!" Hezkale shouts.

"No!" Phoebe cries.

Suddenly, a random idea appears in Phoebe's head, as if she knows exactly what to do. She targets the scepter at those yuets, while envisioning herself in a vast three dimensional 360° protractor with her head positioned in the centre of it. She uses her observational and mathematical strengths enhanced by her autism to aim using a precise geometric angle. "Faseel!" Phoebe shouts. A sharp qwitsul beam of glowing blue light shoots out of the scepter's crystal like a jet with a blasting sound and hits one of the yuets directly in the chest, sending him crashing through the wall behind him, while simultaneously more streams of qwitsuls are absorbed into the scepter's crystal. Phoebe and Hezkale are shocked by the unexpected power of the blast, which even managed to throw off Riddy's flight.

"Hey!" Hezkale says. "I didn't know you were already trained! Why didn't you use the scepter before?!"

Too deep in concentration to give Hezkale a response, she aims the scepter at the last malevolent yuet standing ahead of them. He seems very surprised as he glances at his fallen compatriot, but bravely draws his sword and charges towards them. "Faseel!" Phoebe shouts again. Another beam sends the remaining yuet through a wall. Even though she has no experience fighting with qwitsul magic, she realizes she can use her abilities her autism provides to her benefit.

"Ace!" Phoebe says.

"Superb! Excellent Qelphy!" Hezkale says.

Phoebe and Hezkale change directions, sprinting down the left hall with Riddy winging next to them. Unexpectedly, a muscular yuet man crashes through the ceiling and lands in front of them. He's wielding an overly large scepter in his hand, gripped like a club. Phoebe and Hezkale skid to a halt as the monstrous yuet glares at them. Just before he's about to grab them with his knife-like claws, Phoebe aims the scepter at his head without any hesitation.

"Faseel!" Phoebe shouts. The magic beam's force knocks him out and he tumbles to the floor.

"Superb move Qelphy! Now let's keep going, we're almost there."

They continue racing through the ruined halls and carefully up the broken staircases, as the Xeffizens hunt them. As they both roam around, they behold many threatening sights within the rooms they pass. They see a library going up in flames, centuries of literature feeding the inferno as gigantic yuets drag unconscious smaller yuets with them.

"We're getting closer! Don't stop now!" Hezkale says.

The two of them turn right and left through a couple more paths, before they enter into a tighter hall only to end up at what appears to be a dead end.

"Wrong way!" Phoebe says.

"No, this is right. There's a secret door here," Hezkale explains. "The button is around here somewhere. Help me feel around the wall." Hezkale presses his hands all over the back wall. *A secret door?* She slams her hands against it, playing whack-a-transparent-mole.

"Keep searching, we'll find that button."

"Caught you! You're both trapped!"

Phoebe and Hezkale whirl around. Captain Wazure is leading his pack, with his wide body barely able to fit through the narrow alley, preventing his troops from squeezing past him. To Phoebe's shock, the wound on Wazure's leg is completely healed up. *How'd he heal his wound so fast?!* Phoebe can feel their weight shaking the ground with every step. She points her scepter furiously at Wazure.

"Y-you like to eat? Eat karma! Faseel!" Phoebe shouts.

The qwitsul magic shoots out from the scepter, but Wazure drops his sword and instantly digs his claws into the walls, holding his ground against the spell's force. Phoebe's jaw drops in disbelief, seeing the magic can't beat his ruthless strength. *He's strong, but I bet his head isn't.* Phoebe glares, aiming the scepter at his head.

"Faseel!" Another beam jets against his head, twisting his neck, making him grunt, but he only cracks his head back into position, continuing onwards.

"The spell isn't working!" Phoebe says.

"Keep casting it!" Hezkale yells. It's still slowing them all down! Riddy, help slow him down further!" Riddy flutters up to Wazure, pecking, scratching, squawking and flapping his wings all over his face. Phoebe repeatedly casts the spell at him, trying not to hurt Riddy, but Wazure and his other hulks continue to hold their ground. They creep ever closer, step by step as each magical shot seems to bounce right off of him.

"When I catch you both, I'm going to feed you two to a large friend of mine!" Wazure is soon close enough for his shadow to engulf them.

"Hurry!" Phoebe cries.

Hezkale lowers his hands and manages to feel the cracks making up a square in the wall. "Got it!" he says, pressing the button.

The entire wall turns, shoving Phoebe and Hezkale into a different room, as Riddy abandons Wazure, reuniting with the kids.

"NO! UISHANOLE!" Wazure shouts. The villains charge but the entrance seals just in time, crashing shut.

Phoebe and Hezkale are now in the dining room, where she had eaten Yorgo's amazing baked goods just hours earlier. *We're in the dining room?* The chairs are tossed all over the place and three of the windows are shattered, but at the very least, they're alone.

"Superb, we should be safe for now," Hezkale says. "I've been told that this hidden door is thick and sturdy enough to be impenetrable by any yuet's strength, including ones as strong as Wazure and his soldiers. Great job on holding them off." He curiously stares at her. "But how did you even cast that spell? Were you really even taught anything about magic yet?"

Phoebe is as confused as Hezkale. *Where did that idea come from and how come it worked perfectly? Now that I think about it, that idea pretty much came to me the same way all the knowledge of the Brimcolf language came to me!*

"Well…I-," Phoebe says, but pauses. She glares at Hezkale, wanting him to give her answers instead. "Who are those yuets?"

Hezkale sighs, rubbing the back of his neck. She can guess he doesn't want to tell her, but she needs to know at once. "We didn't feel you were ready to know who those yuets really are yet, but…They're the Xeffizens. The race we need your help to defeat."

Those monsters are the Xeffizens?! Horrified, Phoebe shakes her head and Hezkale nods his.

"I'm sorry, but it's true." Hezkale says. "Really I am. We should've told you when you asked what they're like. We were really afraid you wouldn't help us if you knew what you were up against early on, but I guess there's no point in hiding them from you anymore."

But…How would I ever defeat all those giants at once?! How will I ever be able to get back home now?!

"Come on Qelphy," Hezkale says. "We have to keep moving before any Xeffizens catch us in here."

The two of them run across the room and exit out into another ravaged hallway with Riddy taking flight by their side. Phoebe hopes they'll survive the treacherous night ahead.

Chapter 12

Hezkale leads Phoebe hastily through the badly damaged hallways. The constant flow of qwitsuls helps the carnage around them to appear less hideous. Mysty is still safely tucked in Phoebe's skirt pocket and Riddy soars high above them, both creatures helping keep watch for danger. Hezkale brakes at two intersecting hallways and sticks out his arm, halting Phoebe.

"Where ar-are we supposed to be going?!" Phoebe asks.

"I'm not sure, but we need to find Cernin! He'll know what to do!"

Phoebe feels even worse at not letting Cernin know she was under her bed. There was no way she would've been able to do so after almost being discovered by the Xeffizens. She had been way too terrified to reveal herself. Abruptly, another sword-wielding Xeffizen materializes out of the shadows. With his sword pointed directly at them, the Xeffizen charges. Phoebe aims her scepter at him and prepares to cast her spell, but then a huge axe blade, five feet long and two feet wide, slices into the wall. It has a magical, glowing cord that seems to be alive with qwitsul magic, and the Xeffizen's skin turns a shade of gray, so light it's practically translucent, as he retreats.

"What was that?" Phoebe says.

"That would be Yorgo's doing," Hezkale says joyously.

"Yorgo?"

Yorgo appears out of the dimness of the passageway. He tugs on the qwitsul cord which speedily retracts until the blade is reattached to the large handle. Lifting the axe over his shoulder, he makes it appear far lighter than it actually is. The handle and the blade of the axe contain unique colourful meandering carvings and painted fractal designs which appear to dance with Yorgo's every move. He glances over at Phoebe and Hezkale as a smile of relief passes across his features. He runs up to them as fast as he can, the beads of sweat glistening on his forehead.

"Hezkale! Qelphy! I'm so relieved you're both all right."

"I'm glad you're all right too," Hezkale says. "Do you know where Cernin is? We're trying to find him."

"Yes I do!" Yorgo says. "He's quite high up in the centre tower. I'll take ya both to him."

Yorgo leads the way down meandering hallways. *This tower is like a maze. How does everyone here know where to go so easily? Do yuets just naturally have superior memories compared to mankind?* Up ahead, they notice two large muscular Xeffizens, wielding massive swords. Their features are so similar they could pass for twins! Raising their swords they point them at Yorgo, each one's movements perfectly complimenting the motions of the other. They effectively block the hallway, preventing the trio from proceeding.

"Hand over the uishanole and we'll let you live!" one of the Xeffizens commands.

"I'll hand ya this!" Yorgo says, snapping back.

Yorgo swings the axe, forcing the huge blade to soar down the hallway. The blade slices through both of the swords and a loud snap can be heard as the blades are disconnected from their handles. The severed blades fall to the ground with a clang, leaving the Xeffizens staring at their now pathetic weapons. Yorgo jerks back on the handle, making the qwitsul chord retract. Just like a striking snake, the deadly blow of his axe is over in a matter of seconds. Without an option, the two Xeffizens drop their severed weaponry, withdrawing hastily.

"No Xeffizen would want to mess with dis chef," Yorgo says showing off his weapon. "Let's proceed!"

As the three of them sprint, Phoebe can tell by the sound of his breathing Yorgo is becoming increasingly short of breath.

"Need t-to slow down Yorgo?" Phoebe asks.

Yorgo laughs as he pants. "I may not be the best at runnin', but I stop running when I want to Qelphy, for I can do anything if I put my weight into it."

They race up to a stained glass wall stretching up to the ceiling at one end of the hallway. Although darkened with age, the picture of the sun and moons are still visible.

"We're right on track. The middle section of the tower is really close," Yorgo says, tapping his finger on the window. He holds up his axe. "Stand back." Phoebe and Hezkale step back as he smashes it with one swipe. "I'll find us a shortcut."

Yorgo pushes the shards of sharp glass aside with his blade and the three of them step forward, peering out through the large hole. They're even higher than before. Looking around she sees that although the Hiljin Tower might appear to be one single tower from the outside, it's actually made up of five circular columns starting halfway up the building, four on each corner and one massive tower, which completely dwarfs the other four towers, in the centre. From the tower they're in, she can see the central tower stretches up much taller than the others. A loud ticking sound can be heard coming from inside the tower and to her surprise its clock features seventeen Brimcolf numbers. It would appear that a typical day on Yuetsion is actually thirty-four hours. *Huh, I thought each gonging for each hour was faster than the hours in my world.* She gazes up scrutinizing the chasm-sized distance between it and the tower they're currently in. *So Cernin is high up in the centre tower? How are we going to reach it?*

From a distance, Phoebe watches as numerous Xeffizens and other yuets fight against each other with swords and scepters. Many yuets are also fighting each other through the shattered windows of the opposing towers. She watches in dismay as the Xeffizens kidnap hundreds of the other yuets.

Observing the Xeffizens more closely, she witnesses them casting beams of a mix of black and dark, blood-red magic at the righteous yuets. *The Xeffizens' magic is dark! Is that even qwitsul magic?!*

Phoebe's surprise increases, seeing the yuets cast other qwitsul magic than just Faseel. She watches as they cast out glowing qwitsul swords of various shimmering altering colourations, measuring four feet long and one foot wide, developing out of their scepters' mineral spheres and wielding them as swords instead of just magical blasters. Some Xeffizens create magic blades too, except their colours are the same as their rays. However, they mostly stick to their regular heftier-sized swords, which they carry effortlessly. She makes out the qwitsul blades sounding of clanging crystals whenever they clash against anything.

To Phoebe's disbelief, she witnesses the yuets creating physical realistic mythical creatures, including winged ones and copies of themselves, joining the battle, entirely made of qwitsuls from their scepters! Phoebe visually measures most of them to be about ten feet tall or wide. The evil ones cast by Xeffizens are of the same black and dark red magic with red eyes, lighter shades on their stomachs and darker shades enveloping their qwitsul bodies' remains, while the good ones formed by other yuets are bright, glowing and colourful, like the unused qwitsuls flowing everywhere. They fight the opposing qwitsul monsters or yuets by physically attacking with their claws, teeth or bladed weaponry made of qwitsuls or by firing qwitsul beams from their mouths, eyes, hands or tails. After some time the radiance of their bodies' dims until they disintegrate, only for them to be cast yet again by yuets. She also notices many of them altering into diverse formations instead of remaining as one. Some of them even split into multiple tinier ones and the littler ones merge together into ten foot-sized qwitsul individuals. What surprises her even more is that she overhears them talking intensely like the yuets. Some of their appearances even agitate Phoebe. Different appearances of the dark qwitsul monsters include a furry female being with a shark-like head, four arms, four legs, four eyes, eight clawed fingers and toes and four lengthy eel-like tails, a black striped alligator monster with one head in front and one behind instead of a tail with several curved horns poking from its back and pointed teeth and claws, a scaly, one-eyed bear-like creature with four piercing saber teeth wielding two vast qwitsul axes and multiple smaller dark qwitsul monsters combine together into a plump, thorn-covered, bladed-toothed, wooden monster with extended vine arms and legs. Samplings of the colourful qwitsul characters are a qwitsul spear wielding, scaly yellow skinned, green bellied, red webbed winged, teal striped, hornless, piercing toothed and clawed dragon-like being with two blue eyes huge enough to nearly cover its head, a double qwitsul sword wielding, violet furred, teal fluffy tailed, white bellied, female fox-like being with pink eyes, orange pupils and three spiraling unicorn-like horns poking out of her head, a wingless, indigo skinned, yellow spotted, dragonfly-like creature with ten elongated magenta spidery legs and an aqua feathered, black billed, white footed and clawed, harpy-like creature with eyes containing sapphire sclera, jade irises and white pupils and with drawn-out glossy silky indigo hair grown from her head.

"H-h-holy ace!" Phoebe says. "Qwitsuls can create those creatures?!"

"Yes," Hezkale says, "they're qwitsul servants."

"Qwitsul servants? What are they?"

"They're servants made entirely of qwitsuls that you cast with minds developed exactly like yours like other qwitsul spells and they serve you and they take on whatever form you picture them to be."

"As in…qwitsuls can literally bring your imaginary friends to life to fight by your side?"

"Yes. Any form and colour you imagine."

Phoebe turns to Hezkale with immeasurable awe. "That's a…dream come true."

"No time for talkin," Yorgo says. "I need help finding the quickest, safest path straightaway."

"Right," Hezkale says.

Observing downwards for the best trail among the brawling yuets and qwitsul servants, a silent feeling of rage and terror builds up inside of Phoebe as she reaches the conclusion she's powerless to stop what's going on. She feels the most shaken she's ever felt to witness the treachery of a real-life battle. Gazing down to her left, she gasps, the once beautiful garden Hilmina and Hezkale had shown her is going up in flames. Tears trickle down her cheeks, as everything she treasured, especially the gilgo berry tree, the best bird feeder she had ever beheld, slowly disappears in a sea of flames.

"This intrusion is far worse than I thought. It appears the path ahead is our only choice to reach Cernin. Both of ya back up," Yorgo says.

Yorgo flings his axe across the wide chasm. It sticks into the bottom jaw of a monstrous-looking statue's gaping mouth on the side of the centre tower. He tugs at the chord a few times; making sure the blade is firmly attached to the statue.

"That should do. We're going ta have to swing to the centre tower," Yorgo says.

"Huh?!" Phoebe says in shock.

Hezkale slips his swords into his belt and wraps his arms around Yorgo's left arm. Yorgo offers Phoebe his other hand, but she backs away.

"No! I-I can't!" Phoebe cries, pressing her back against the wall.

"You must Qelphy! It's our only chance!" Yorgo explains, but she backs away further overtaken by fear. "Listen, I'm much stronger than I look. If I can wield my axe, I can easily hold onto you and I'll never let you fall."

"It will be alright. We promise you," Hezkale says.

Unfortunately, more Xeffizens arrive at the very end of the hall they're inside. The middle one points at Phoebe. "There they are!" Phoebe stares at them in alarm. She doesn't know which is worse, swinging over deadly depths or being captured by the Xeffizens. One of the Xeffizens pulls a round object from his belt pocket. It's a steel orb with a top consisting of reflective chrome and symbols along the equator.

"Trust me Qelphy!" Yorgo says. "Remember I said that I can do anything if I put my weight into it! I'm also as afraid as you are, if it makes ya feel any better!"

Phoebe looks at Yorgo. Her eyes dart swiftly back and forth between his hand and the Xeffizens behind them. She takes a deep breath. "I do trust you." Yorgo gazes down at her and smiles, reaching out his hand as the Xeffizen pitches the object towards them. Hearing it bouncing, Yorgo grabs Phoebe's waist and completely lifts her up off the ground. Phoebe gasps, feeling her chest tighten. Something tells her she's about to have the most dangerous ride of her life. She can feel Mysty digging her claws into her side.

Without hesitation, Yorgo leaps right out of the tower. Riddy, shrieking angrily, soars behind them. With wind gusts blowing, an enormous explosion blows up the entire section of the tower they were just standing in. The tower's statues, stone walls and windows collapse as the three of them swing downwards. The debris rains out over the fighting below. Phoebe can't even find the strength to cry out in fear. All she finds herself able to do is wrap her arms tightly around Yorgo's thick neck. With the keen timing skills her autism provides, she can tell if they had waited even another few seconds to jump, they would've been entangled in the debris from the explosion.

As they swing below the statue, Yorgo's axe begins to slip. Their combined weight is too much and it pulls the blade out of the statue. Phoebe lets out a silent scream as they plunge down to the fighting below. Yorgo angles his body in an effort to aim the trio towards a vast stained glass window. The three of them crash through the window, but Yorgo takes most of the impact and manages to set Phoebe and Hezkale safely onto the ground. He stands up and works the kinks out of his back.

"You did great Qelphy," Yorgo says.

Phoebe nods, reflecting back on the deadly explosion they had just narrowly survived. She checks her pocket and sees Mysty is still tucked inside of it, unhooking her claws from her clothing. To settle her down, she gives Mysty's shaken head a quick rub. She glances around the room they've entered into. Numerous chairs and tables hug the sides of the room. Long thick drapes, almost touching the ground, hang from the walls and windows. Three vast stained glass windows, the middle one being broken thanks to them, give the room the feeling of being inside of a kaleidoscope.

"Now that we're safely in the main tower, all we need to do is head upwards," Yorgo says. "We should meet Cernin up there."

The large double doors swing open, reverberating with a loud bang. Hezkale and Yorgo point their weapons towards the doors and encourage Phoebe to do the same. Twenty Xeffizens armed with swords and glowing scepters pour into the room. Half of them are male and the other half female. Like the men, Xeffizen women have no hair, but unlike the men, they also wear black cloth wrapped around their chests. They back away, knowing they have no chance of fighting against so many all at once. Mysty pokes her head out of Phoebe's skirt pocket and hisses at the Xeffizens. Riddy squawks aggressively.

"There are more yuets over there," says one of the Xeffizen men. He pulls out his large scepter and smiles. "Let's seize them."

The Xeffizens begin to walk towards them. *How are we going to fight them?! There's too many!*

"I know that we're outnumbered, but we have to do something," Hezkale tells Phoebe.

Phoebe shakily keeps her scepter aimed at the Xeffizens, who are slowly closing the gap between them.

"Put down yer weapons," says a Xeffizen. "Ya aready know yer outcome."

A musical melody echoes throughout the chamber. The Xeffizens pause and glance around, wondering where the music is coming from. Even Phoebe and Hezkale are confused by this sudden interruption. The tension in the room seems to lessen as the music overtakes their senses.

Phoebe, who's really good with music, can easily identify instruments by listening to their sounds and vibrations. After a few seconds of listening, she identifies the sounds of a harp playing somewhere nearby.

"What's that noise?" a Xeffizen woman asks.

In sync with the music, thin strands of glowing streams of qwitsul magic wrap around the tables and chairs, lifting them into the air. Everyone is startled by the qwitsuls lifting the objects, meaning they're being cast. Everyone, that is, except Yorgo and Hezkale. In fact, they appear to be enjoying it. The Xeffizens aim their weapons at the floating objects.

"Qwitsul magic! Who's castin' it?!" shouts a Xeffizen man, as tables and chairs crash into his companions. They fall one by one, failing to duck out of the way. Phoebe, Hezkale and Yorgo hurriedly sink down and lay their bodies flat against the ground, shielding their heads with their hands for added protection. Riddy huddles next to Hezkale. Phoebe covers her head and neck as the chaos ensues above. In an attempt to stave off the assault, the Xeffizens swing their weapons and aim their scepters, but the furniture's movements are too unpredictable. After all the Xeffizens have been knocked unconscious, the music ceases, dissipating the qwitsul strands and dropping the furniture.

"My, my. What would you do without me?" says a familiar voice.

Huh? That voice...

A yuet woman enters into the room from behind a curtain covering up the doorway to another room. The woman steps into the moonlight. Hilmina stands before them holding a glossy obsidian-like harp with thin well-carved rims decked with an assortment of multi-coloured glowing minerals. The instrument is almost as tall as she is. The strings sparkle and glimmer, seeming to dance in an elaborate pattern like all the other minerals. It's the most stunning instrument Phoebe has ever seen.

"There's a reason why the yuets I know call me 'The Queen of Music'," Hilmina says, placing her hand on her hip.

"Hilmina!" Yorgo runs up to Hilmina and hugs her tightly causing her to drop the harp. He lifts her up off the floor, twirls her around and kisses her on the lips. "Perfect timing Hilmina! I'm so glad yer safe."

"I'm glad you're all safe too," Hilmina says, letting go of Yorgo and picking up her harp. "Are you alright Qelphy and Hezkale?"

Phoebe slowly nods her head as she stares incredulously at Hilmina's harp. *Hilmina made all of that furniture move? How did she do it? Did she do it all by playing that harp? How does that work? How does she control qwitsul magic from it? How does she even manage to carry it so easily?*

"We're fine," Hezkale says, as Riddy perches on his head. "Is Cernin here?"

"Yes he is. He's up near the tower's clock," Hilmina says, pointing upwards.

"Let's go then!" Yorgo says.

The four of them hurry out of the room, abandoning all of the comatose Xeffizens. Soaring high above, Riddy follows them. They sprint down demolished hallways and gingerly trace their way up dozens of flights of cracked staircases. They see five Xeffizens vandalizing the halls and snagging a pair of helpless Veshaels, who are trying to punch them.

"I'll deal with them," Hilmina says, holding up her harp.

Hilmina begins playing her harp, creating multiple strands of qwitsul magic from its strings which envelope a chair, a fallen door and the snapped rims of a painting, allowing them to magically float into the air and repeatedly hit the Xeffizens' bodies, forcing them to unhand the Veshaels. Fascinated, Phoebe observes the way Hilmina fights. She watches Hilmina grip the harp's rim with one hand, while playing it with the other. Apparently, her harp can control qwitsul magic with the ability to lift up loose objects and move them wherever she wants slowly or briskly, depending on the musical rhythm she strums. Her musical talent allows her to tame vicious opponents without so much as lifting a finger. The two Veshaels wave appreciatively at Hilmina as they rush down the hallway in the opposite direction. Hilmina quickly finishes off the Xeffizens, knocking them unconscious with a swift smack against the heavy door.

The group keeps moving—they know the Xeffizens are everywhere. Phoebe can see them in the rooms as they rush by. An air of discouragement begins to descend upon everyone as they realize there's no safe place to hide. Phoebe feels a sense of helplessness as she watches yuets being attacked physically or magically and seized by the Xeffizens. They dash towards a tremendously wide staircase within a spacious area where numerous regular sized yuets and Xeffizens brawl against each other with swords, scepters, qwitsul blades and various qwitsul servants. Astonishingly, she witnesses some of the qwitsul servants morphing their arms and tails into bladed qwitsuls, using them to physically fight against their adversaries. The qwitsul forces of the scepters shove the yuets over the stair banisters to fall down to the floor below. Some of the yuets tumble down the stairs, toppling others below them. The qwitsul servants impaled or sliced by bladed weaponry or struck by magic, sending them airborne or knocking them off the steps, dissipate in defeat. The four of them come to a halt. They know the risk involved in ascending up those chaotic stairs. Riddy perches on Phoebe's shoulder, which would normally cheer her up, but she's too focused on what's unfolding before her to pay attention. Mysty meows, patting her paws against Phoebe's side.

Phoebe's eyes widen in fascination, seeing the yuets fire minor beams, which create bulky glowing crystals made of qwitsuls from their scepters and qwitsul servants form minerals from themselves too, developing ten foot mineral peaks and abstract splash formations, jingling and clattering during every production. Like the other qwitsul spells, the qwitsul gems come in any lovely colour casted by the virtuous combatants and the gleaming magical stones created by the villainous battlers have the murky red coat. In different angles, they use them to freeze their opponents in place, force them down or off the stairway or impale the qwitsul servants, disintegrating their bodies. *Creating crystals with qwitsuls too?! Wait, I've seen Princess Vehilia do this same thing in that mirror labyrinth!*

"How are we going to make it through all of this?!" Hezkale asks.

"I can't swing all of us up there," Yorgo says.

Hilmina inspects the area and detects a large flat broken chunk of the glassy stone wall, lying on the ground behind them. Her eyes widen as a smirk spreads across her face. "I have an idea." She jogs back and leaps onto the fallen wall. She strums her harp, encompassing the wall with qwitsul magic, lifting it off the ground, like a hovering flying saucer, over to them. "Get on." Phoebe, Hezkale and Yorgo jump onto the floating platform and they all crouch down onto their knees to keep their stability.

"Superb idea!" Yorgo says.

Hilmina continues to control their platform as it swiftly rises above the stairs. Instead of flying next to them, Riddy stays grounded, clenching his feet into Phoebe's clothing. The chaos on the stairs continues as they rise on their makeshift flying carpet. She can see they're stealing the attention of a few of the Xeffizens and their qwitsul servants from the fighting, but luckily most of them are too pre-occupied with battling the yuets to pitch their swords or cast magic from their scepters at the escapees. They soar all the way to the top of the stairs, through the vast entrance and down more chaotic hallways. More Xeffizens and dark qwitsul servants notice them coming and cast dusky beams at them. The malicious qwitsul servants with webbed or feathered wings, taking on forms closest to an evil three lion-like headed dragon, a stalk eyed and two tailed merman, winged Xeffizens, a bat-like being with five tentacle legs, an oversized scaly gorilla-like monster's head with wings and more, even begin fluttering after them.

"Hang on," yells Hilmina, as Hezkale cheers. She swishes their platform, dodging the magic beams and qwitsul servants' attacks. A few rays hit their intended target, breaking off small pieces and latching a couple unpleasant crystals onto their ride near Phoebe, triggering her scream. She shudders as she feels the platform crumble. Hilmina has maintained such a precise control over her subjects before, it's scary to see her start faltering now. Riddy detaches himself from Phoebe, swerving downwards, pecking, scratching, squawking and distracting the Xeffizens below and the qwitsul servants above.

"Qelphy! I need you to help stop our foes from attacking us!" Hilmina says.

"What?! But I'll fall off if I do!"

She would try to cast magic at the enemies, but she's too afraid to let go of the platform. It wouldn't take much for her to lose her balance.

"Hold onto my tail! I won't let you fall off!" Yorgo says.

Phoebe wonders if holding onto Yorgo's tail will make a difference, but nonetheless she grabs it with her free hand. This is not the time for questioning. His tail, remarkably more flexible than it appears, wraps around her arm like a tight rope, helping Phoebe feel secure, even if he's touching her. She aims her scepter, concentrating on the Xeffizens with scepters and their qwitsul servants.

"Faseel!" She casts a magic beam at one of the attacking Xeffizens, flinging him across the combating yuets. She uses the keen timing skills her autism provides to anticipate the speed they're going, casting at critical moments and capitalizes upon her precise math skills to correctly angle and aim her scepter. She successfully fires at a good number of the attacking qwitsul servants, defeating and evaporating them. She even manages deflecting some of their magic attacks with her own, generating thunderous fireworks of intermixed light and dark magic. Phoebe's ears ring from their percussions. Hilmina veers sharply to the left down yet another hallway. As their ride turns sharply, Phoebe swerves outwards off their platform, making her shriek, but Yorgo's strong tail pulls her back onto its surface, just before she collides into a wall.

"Don't worry Qelphy! I'm not letting ya go!" Yorgo says.

"You're doing amazing Qelphy! Don't stop now!" Hezkale says.

"R-r-right," Phoebe says, refocusing on the Xeffizens.

Phoebe casts more magic at the aggressive Xeffizens, shoving them into walls and across the hall hitting the floor in an attempt to knock them out and qwitsul servants, blotting them out when beaten. She even manages to hit some of the crystal orbs of the Xeffizens' scepters, exploding them into bits with qwitsuls oozing out and other qwitsuls getting absorbed back into their crystal shards, meaning the Xeffizens' dark-looking magic must be qwitsul magic too, but in an opposing form. The reduced numbers of the enemy allow a significant number of the minor yuets to be freed from certain captivity. They abandon most of the Xeffizens and their qwitsul partners they soar over, before any opportunities to attack can present themselves.

As they coast up the staircases and down the hallways, heading higher and higher up into the tower, the number of Xeffizens begins to decline. They start to reach areas where no signs of battle can be seen. The halls are in pristine condition and are quite a contrast to the demolished floors lower down. *Have we finally lost the Xeffizens?* Their magic hovercraft decelerates and descends towards the ground.

"I can't play anymore. I need a break," Hilmina says.

They land on the ground as the platform slides across the hall finally coming to a complete stop as the friction of the floor brakes their forward momentum. Riddy sets down on Phoebe's shoulder, chirping in a relieved tone. The four of them step off the hovercraft and quickly continue climbing ever higher to the top of the tower. The walls are decorated with velvet hangers displaying golden, scaly hound-like creatures akin to golveys, sitting upright like poised warriors. It would appear the fighting has yet to claim this section of the tower.

"S-Say," Phoebe pants, "the magic the Xeffizens attacked us with w-were…darker, more menacing colours. Were those qwitsuls too?"

"Yes, qwitsuls could be used for good reasons or bad reasons," Hezkale explains, "depending on what kind of yuet uses them. Remember when I told you that the qwitsuls you mentally communicate with when spellcasting develop minds and intentions exactly like your own as part of the spellcasting process? The Xeffizens casting dark qwitsuls is a good example of that. The magic is bright and colourful when yuets with good intentions spell cast them and dark when yuets with bad intentions spell cast them, including magic cast as qwitsul servants. Since the Xeffizens use the qwitsuls for evil intentions, they become dark and ugly because they develop the Xeffizens' dark mindsets and intentions and then become neutral minded again, back in their beautiful, colourful forms, only dimmer when their powers are fully used up from the spellcasting process. Your mind is the key to their powers."

"Now it makes sense," Phoebe says.

At last, they come across Cernin who's directing the dependable yuets up the vast finely carved stone staircase. It spirals upwards towards the gigantic clock tower high above. Phoebe sighs in relief. Cernin notices them coming towards him and waves enthusiastically.

"Qelphy! Hezkale! Hilmina! Yorgo!" Cernin says, looking excited and relieved. "I'm so glad the four of you are safe."

"Yeah, so are we and we're glad you're good too. Have ya seen any Xeffizens around here?" Yorgo asks in a serious tone.

"So far no," Cernin says. "That's the last of the yuets who've managed to make it this far. We have to hurry up to the top too and protect Qelphy!"

Without another word the five of them race hurriedly up yet another flight of stairs. Phoebe peeks downwards over the banister. This section of the tower appears to be an endless drop beneath them. Cernin halts at the top of the first set of stairs.

"Why are you stopping?" Hezkale asks.

"I'm making sure those Xeffizens won't follow us."

He pulls out a two-foot long bronze gun of some sort, which features glass orbs filled with blue, whitish-yellow and dark brown fluids. He points the gun at the middle of the stairs they've just scaled and flicks a switch. He fires one of the brown orbs at the stairs and it explodes, startling everyone, except Cernin. The flight of stairs collapses.

Cernin raises his gun, adjusts his monocle and smiles. "That should slow them down. Off we go!"

As they hustle, they start to hear shouts echoing from further below. They glance down. It appears the Xeffizens have made it up as far as the damaged staircase.

"Don't worry," Cernin says. "That's as far as they can get."

"Could their flying qwitsul servants c-c-carry them up?" Phoebe asks.

"Oh, their normal-sized qwitsul servants aren't big enough to carry their weight."

But the Xeffizens stab their claws roughly into the interior walls and begin to climb.

"Oh dear!" Hilmina says.

Cernin shoots continuously at the staircases below. As they sprint higher, they come across rotating and ticking gears ranging in size from small to huge along the walls. They're all interconnected to each other over the massive clockworks suspended in the middle of the tower. They even pass by the giant swinging clock pendulum, its constant ticking echoing loudly throughout the tower. *The ticking is getting louder, so we must be getting closer!* Phoebe peeks down again and watches as the Xeffizens continue to climb. *Those Xeffizens are going to get us! They're even going to get all the other yuets here! If they get me, then I'll never be able to go back home! I...I must do something, dream or not!*

Phoebe stops running and puts her strong observation skills to use. Cernin, Hezkale, Hilmina and Yorgo stop too while Riddy perches himself onto the handrail of the staircase eyeing Phoebe with concern. "What are you doing?!" Cernin says. "You can't stop now!"

Phoebe ignores Cernin and scrutinizes the gears. Catching sight of something promising, she looks directly at some bolts holding up a very huge gear above the massive machinery. *Hmm, if I shoot that gear down, it may cause all the other gears to collapse onto the Xeffizens below us!* She tries to aim the scepter directly at the bolts, hoping the force of the qwitsul magic will shove the bolts out of the large gear. Next, she puts her math skills to use, specifically geometry, angling the scepter in such a way by envisioning mathematical angles with her imaginary protractor simultaneously; the qwitsuls' vigour will hopefully push the bolts out.

"Qelphy?" Hezkale asks, wondering what Phoebe's planning to do.

Unexpectedly, the ground vibrates and cracks near Phoebe's feet, as they hear a punching sound. The floor cracks open and a Xeffizen's large clawed hand smashes through the stairs, snatching Phoebe's ankle. Phoebe trips from the Xeffizen's pull and screams. The hand starts tugging her down, as she struggles to hold onto something. In great terror, Cernin, Yorgo, Hezkale and Hilmina clutch onto Phoebe's hands, her scepter and one another, attempting to pull her back up, but the Xeffizen dragging her down is stronger than all of them combined. Phoebe shrieks from the pain in her ankle, as the Xeffizen grips and tugs it tightly. She looks up at the others and sees they're as panicked as she is. In this state, all she can do is stare back in terror.

"Help!" Phoebe cries.

"Don't let her go!" Cernin shouts.

Mysty leaps out of Phoebe's skirt pocket and bites the Xeffizen's hand. The Xeffizen below shouts in pain and smacks Mysty up into the air with his other hand. "Mysty!" Phoebe screams, but luckily Mysty claws and clenches onto Yorgo's tail, making him yell in pain.

The Xeffizen yanks Phoebe's ankle hard, effectively jerking Phoebe out of the hands of her protectors and forces her hand to slip away from her scepter.

"NO!" Hezkale shouts.

The Xeffizen wraps his thick muscular arm firmly around Phoebe. Phoebe looks into his face and gasps. It's Captain Wazure!

"Did you miss me?" Wazure asks. Phoebe screams as Wazure slides down the wall by digging his claws into it. The shrill noise of claws on stone is almost deafening. He lands on a set of stairs, which had missed being damaged by Cernin's explosives. Horrified, Phoebe never thought her nightmares of being kidnapped by monsters would literally come true.

"You're coming with me, uishanole," Wazure says.

"Wazure! Don't you dare touch her!" Hilmina furiously demands.

"I'll chop off your tail and head if you harm her!" Yorgo shouts, raising his axe.

Wazure stares up at them in irritation. "Shut up! If any of you attack me or follow me, I'll bite this girl's head off!" He looks straight into Phoebe's eyes up close. "And if you don't give me any more trouble, I just might be considerate enough to spare your weak life, until our king decides to kill you instead."

"No!" Phoebe cries.

Hezkale, Hilmina, Cernin, Yorgo, Riddy and Mysty gaze helplessly down. Phoebe shakily examines Wazure's sharp teeth, which do indeed look big and piercing enough to chomp her head off. He's holding her close enough to smell his toxic breath, which smells of rotten fish, cow tongue and molasses. Having never been this close to a Xeffizen before, Phoebe tries to avoid eye contact and takes one more desperate glance towards her trustworthy yuets. She feels like she's about to cry, figuring she's doomed, but she stops herself. She remembers how much she desires to get back home to be reunited with her family and that's exactly what she'll do. *No! I'm going home no matter what!* She begins pushing, smacking and hitting Wazure's face with her fists, which doesn't seem to hurt his thick skull much, but it definitely aggravates him.

"HEY!" Wazure shouts. "Why you…"

His grip on Phoebe's back grows tighter as his claws get dangerously close to piercing her skin. Phoebe repeatedly cries out, gasps and cringes from the pain in her back. Unable to bare the pain or the fact she's most likely about to get stabbed by what feels like five knives, she whistles noisily near Wazure's ear, hoping he'll release her to cover his ears. She has sensitive hearing, but she's definitely used to her own loudness. Normally she whistles loudly to get her parent's or any bird's attention, if they're too far away to be heard by her voice. Wazure grunts and uses his free hand to block his ear. *He can't handle my loud whistling!* Phoebe gets an idea, thinking there may be a speck of hope after all. She whistles louder. He groans and growls louder from the pain Phoebe's screeching whistling is causing. He unplugs his earhole and tries covering her mouth with his palm, but she chomps his hand the hardest ever, making him roar in agony. He yanks his hand away, allowing her to proceed whistling.

Wazure finally drops Phoebe onto the stairs. She manages to land on her feet and hands. Since his substantial body is blocking her path, Phoebe runs through his legs. He lowers his fat tail, and twists it around her belly. She finds herself desperate to scream, but instead whistles loudly once more. Wazure shrieks, shielding his ears again. Her distraction forces his tail to loosen its constrictive grip. She quickly squeezes herself out of it.

"Quick Qelphy! Come closer to us!" Hezkale says, detecting an opportunity.

Phoebe deserts Wazure, running to the end of the damaged stairs, which is as close as she can get to the trusted yuets. Glancing down, she sees hundreds of Xeffizens climbing the walls and clockworks towards her. One of them snickers threateningly at her, holding a saliva smothered sword in his mouth. She gasps, backing away from the horrible sight. She feels a thudding vibration in the stairs growing increasingly stronger. Peering over her shoulder, she sees Wazure furiously charging with his claws directed at her. She whistles again, causing him to shout and plug his ears, making sure he doesn't come any closer.

What do I do now?! I can't whistle forever!

"Lower me down Hilmina!" Hezkale yells, gripping his swords firmly. Hilmina strums her harp with the qwitsul strands wrapping around and raising Hezkale's swords into the air, as he holds onto them. With Hilmina's help,

Hezkale glides down to the ground in front of Phoebe, surprising her. "Quick, grab onto my back!" Hearing Hilmina playing her harp above and noticing magic swirling around the swords, Phoebe comprehends what Hezkale plans to do. She scrambles onto his back, distracting Wazure with her whistling as Hezkale raises his swords.

"Now Hilmina!" Hezkale yells.

Hilmina plays her harp faster, miraculously lifting Hezkale's swords, which pull Hezkale and Phoebe into the air. They soar up towards the stairs above.

"No!" Wazure jumps and reaches for Phoebe's feet, but he only accomplishes snagging the heel part of one of her socks. He crashes back down onto the stairs and roars in anger. Phoebe hugs Hezkale tightly, and they both float back onto the stairs where Hilmina, Cernin and Yorgo are. Hilmina stops playing and Hezkale sheaths his swords. The orange tabby meows joyfully at the safe return of her friend and Phoebe tucks her back into her skirt pocket.

"Great thinking Hezkale!" Cernin praises. "Now let's go! We still might have enough time to leave!"

Phoebe shakes her head and snatches her scepter up from where it had been lying on the stairs. She aims it directly at the bolts.

"Reinforce me with qwitsul servants! Get the uishanole!" Wazure shouts at the Xeffizens below.

The Xeffizens below cast out hundreds of winged dark qwitsul servants, taking on appearances similar to a winged scaly tiger with ten legs containing lengthy claws, a finless liopleurodon with four spiked webbed wings with two curved horns formed from its nose, a couple wyvern-like creatures with one being spotted and single headed and the other striped and four headed, a five horned pterodactyl-like being, a huge bat with a single eyed lizard-like head, a furred, eight armed and wolf-like headed gargoyle, a beautiful yet dark female fairy with wild prolonged hair and so on, from their scepters. They soar upwards around the clockworks towards Phoebe, but she chooses to ignore them, especially since she doesn't find them and the Xeffizens as threatening as the mirror labyrinth monster.

"We'll chew you to pieces uishanole!" shouts the adult male voiced grinning liopleurodon-like qwitsul servant.

"Qelphy! We don't have time-!" Yorgo says.

"Faseel!" Phoebe shouts. A magic beam blasts directly at the bolts, shoving them out of place a bit. "Faseel! Faseel! Faseel!" She confidently repeats the spell until the bolts finally push completely out. The giant gear creaks as it slowly tilts and instantly collapses. The hefty force of its weight causes most of the gears, the giant pendulum and the other clock tower parts to break off and collapse downwards. An avalanche of metal machinery rains down on the panicked qwitsul servants, crushing them with their weight and fading them, and the Xeffizens, forcing them to loosen their grips on the walls. One by one they plummet downwards into the tower's depths along with the enormous clock parts. Phoebe, Hezkale, Hilmina, Cernin, Yorgo and Wazure watch in shock as the Xeffizens scream, tumbling hundreds of feet below until they fade from sight.

"Ace," Phoebe says.

Wazure claws onto the wall and slides rapidly downwards into the dark chasm below. "Look!" Hilmina says. Wazure vanishes into the distance.

"He got away," Yorgo says.

"Nothing we can do about it," Cernin says. "Come on, we'd better hurry."

The five of them continue running up the stairs with Riddy hitching a ride on Hezkale's shoulder and Phoebe slipping Mysty into her pocket. They head towards the top of the clock tower. Echoing far below them, they hear Wazure shouting and roaring angrily at the top of his lungs.

"UISHANOLE…!"

Chapter 13

Phoebe is the first to reach the top step of the clock tower, Mysty poking out from her skirt pocket. Hezkale, Hilmina, Yorgo and Cernin follow breathlessly. They enter an enormous room filled with yuets of all ages. As the five of them squeeze through the crush, Phoebe glances towards the gigantic glass face of the clock at the other end of the room. It's the most impressive clock she has ever seen. *Ace!*

Phoebe's fascination with clocks began at a very young age. One aspect of her autism is a focus on order and to her clocks, with their intricate gears and the numbers on their faces, has always been a good representative of that. They continue to keep accurate time long after everything around them has descended into chaos. When she was younger, she and her parents would deliberately stop by the clock store just to gaze at them (she still does once in a while).

Hefty gears and other clock parts are attached to the walls and pillars by enormous bolts and the abstract structures of clockworks in the centre areas of the room are guarded by stone handrails. Eight hefty purple oval crystals attached to the ceiling provide light, letting everyone see where they're going and rendering the qwitsuls invisible. Phoebe and the others traipse up a few stairs to a platform where a Kume man wearing a strange outfit stands. To Phoebe, the outfit looks like something a captain in the military would wear.

"We're here with the uishanole, captain," Cernin says.

"Excellent, we're prepared Cernin," says the Kume Captain. "Care to do the honours Hilmina?"

Prepared for what?

Hilmina nods and strums her fingers across the strings of her harp. The qwitsul magic created by her instrument forms streams through the fractured glass of the clock's face and strings itself onto the ends of the two gigantic clock hands simultaneously shifting them in opposite directions. The hands appear to be producing some type of pattern. Whenever they both halt at a Brimcolf number set, she changes their directions, moving them to a different pair of numbers. Phoebe watches in astonishment as Hilmina controls the two vast clock hands with very little effort. The hands are so vast and heavy Phoebe is sure not even an Olympic weight lifter would've been able to move them. The hands start to strike midnight, being number seventeen, as a final chord from the harp makes them meet together once again. The entire area begins to vibrate.

Phoebe grabs onto a handrail. *Now what's happening?!* Every single gear and clock mechanism separates from its neighbour. The pieces of the clock switch positions and reconnect with completely different mechanisms. Phoebe looks over at the windows and observes four oversized steel wings unfurling from within the clock tower's head. Two massive steel propellers unfold themselves at the front edge of each wing. The entire chamber tilts back and forth, encouraging yuets to hang on to whatever and whoever's closest to them. It's as if they were expecting this to happen. Phoebe looks through one of the windows of the clock's face and discovers the entire clock head is raising right off its body! They're floating up into the sky!

The sound of an activating engine reverberates from way back inside, but at least the discordant noise isn't too much for Phoebe to endure. She watches increduously as immense units of the clock tower's outer walls crumble and fall off. The tower's head hovers higher into the atmosphere as its load is significantly lightened.

"What is this?!" Phoebe asks Cernin.

Cernin looks at her and grins. "This was a clock tower, but now it's an airship."

Phoebe's eyes widen in bewilderment. "An airship? A flying ship?"

Cernin nods.

Phoebe rushes up to the glass face of the clock tower and stares through it. Being so high up in the air is making her feel lightheaded. Gazing upwards, she spots the tips of two colossal revolving propellers, pushing them higher into the sky. The engine creates a different sound and the ship drifts forward. It gradually increases its speed the further it gets from the tower. Now that they're safely out of the grasp of the Xeffizens, the airborne yuets let out an enthusiastic cheer. Phoebe winces and plugs her ears as their cries grow even louder. She glances over at the wings and notices numerous smaller rotating propellers which are slowly pulling them away from the remnants of the clock tower. She gazes ahead, trying to keep everything she has experienced straight in her head. *The head of the clock tower was an airship the entire time? How is that even possible?*

Phoebe runs along the wall, away from the overjoyed crowd of yuets, to another window. She watches as the distance between the airship and the tower increases with every rotation of the propellers. The remainders of the tower have been engulfed in flames. She gapes at the intense structure now in danger of collapse. Her mind has been caught completely unaware by the fact they truly made it through the structure to the top. They had practically been kissing death at every turn. *That could have been us in that tower...Hopefully all of the other good yuets are all right...*

"Fly into those clouds up ahead," Cernin says. "That way, the Xeffizens won't be able to see where we're headed."

The Kume Captain clutches the steering wheel and coaxes the airship up into the clouds, obstructing Phoebe's view of the Hiljin tower.

"May I have everyone's attention please?!" Cernin announces.

All the yuets turn and focus their attention on Cernin. Hezkale walks up to Phoebe, who's still worrying about the good yuets left behind at the Hiljin Tower and stolen by the Xeffizens, with Riddy still perched on his shoulder.

"Come along. Cernin is about to make a speech," Hezkale says.

They squeeze a path through the yuet pack and join Hilmina and Yorgo, who are standing at Cernin's side. He removes his monocle and gazes out over the crowd.

"I am…terribly sorry for the dangers we've gone through tonight," Cernin says. "I had no idea that the Xeffizens would attack us…The only reason the Xeffizens would attack us now would be because they suspect we have plans to save Yuetsion. I don't know how the Xeffizens got wind of our plans."

Phoebe's eyes widen as she remembers the conversation she overheard between Wazure and his soldiers about how the Xeffizens had figured out their plans. She feels a strong urge to explain to him what she knows, but she's far too shy to speak up in front of such a vast gathering.

"It's most likely that spies working for King Zexen discovered our plans, so we must be extremely cautious with our surroundings. But the worst part about tonight is that the Xeffizens have captured more than a thousand of our supporters." The yuets begin to mutter amongst themselves. The tension in the air is so thick it has an almost tangible feel to it. Cernin raises his hand, hushing them. "However, we commend them for their bravery in helping to fight off the Xeffizens for us. We shall be forever in their debt. Unfortunately, the loss of these volunteers means that from this point on, we need to take matters into our own hands. I feel that this is what our stolen yuets would want us to do."

The yuets nod their heads in agreement.

"But that doesn't mean we have lost hope. As long as the uishanole is by our side, we may still possibly have the power to save the captured yuets and Yuetsion itself from those dreadful Xeffizens. However…unfortunately, since they've discovered the existence of our uishanole, our journey is going to be much harder than we had anticipated. The Xeffizens will stop at nothing to get their hands on her. So we must be willing to persevere as we continue our fight against the Xeffizens. Qelphy, our uishanole, will need our full protection from beginning to end! Our journey to save Yuetsion…begins now!"

As everyone cheers, Cernin gestures towards Phoebe. The deafening noise from so many yuets applauding forces Phoebe to shield her ears again. Hezkale leads Phoebe up to the top of the stairs next to the ship's wheel, letting everyone catch sight of her. Being made visible to such a huge group, who are depending on her to rescue their world, causes unlimited discomfort for Phoebe. She doesn't even have the courage to bow. All she's capable of doing is standing there as silent as a statue. Cernin slips his monocle back onto his face and raises his hand again, in an effort to silence the crowd. "We have a long day tomorrow, so let's all get as much rest as we can."

The yuets gradually leave the wheel room through its numerous entryways. Mysty meows and begins to climb out of the safety of her pocket. Phoebe carefully helps her out of the pocket and gently places her on the floor. She taps Cernin on the shoulder capturing his attention.

"Yes Qelphy?" Cernin asks.

"I-I remember overhearing Wazure…talking about how they figured out your plans to save Yuetsion," Phoebe says.

Cernin, Hilmina, Hezkale, Yorgo and even the Kume Captain all gape at her in surprise.

"You did?!" Yorgo asks.

"How did they do it?!" Cernin asks.

Phoebe steps away from their overwhelming intensity. "I-I heard him say they captured a number of y-yuets from your group because they thought it-it was strange that so many yuets were meeting at the Hiljin Tower. The Xeffizens then forced them to tel-tell them what's going on."

Cernin rubs his chin in astonishment. "Hmm, so they suspected us long before they knew about our plans. They're a lot craftier than we predicted. We probably should've limited our volunteer intake in an effort to become less noticeable."

"Too late for that now," Hezkale says.

"But that's very good information to know. Thank you very much Qelphy, you brilliant alien you," Cernin says.

"My, my, I guess this means we have to constantly watch our backs to make sure no Xeffizens are stalking us," Hilmina says.

Phoebe stares down at the ground, gripping her arm. The power of the fear residing within her is on a level she has never felt before. Mysty rubs her head against Phoebe's foot, but it's not enough to provide the comfort she's seeking.

"Don't worry Qelphy, I assure you you're well-protected," Cernin says in an uplifting voice, "and knowing the way you think and fight, you're going to do excellent on our journey."

"We'll always be here for you Qelphy," Hezkale says.

Phoebe nods, but her feelings of inadequacy don't seem to be fading.

"You'll probably feel better after a good night's rest," Cernin says. "There's still seven more hours until the morning sun rises. Hilmina? Would you kindly show Qelphy to her new bedroom?"

"Sure thing Cernin," Hilmina says. "Follow me Qelphy."

Hilmina motions Phoebe to follow her. Mysty trots briskly by Phoebe's side. Phoebe glances back and catches Hezkale giving her a friendly wave and Riddy whistling pleasantly from his shoulder. She gives them a slight smile, but she's too shaken to wave back at them.

"I'll meet ya in our room!" Yorgo calls.

Phoebe follows Hilmina as she looks for an available room for her. The hallways are almost perfectly symmetrical, with glowing blue crystals embedded into the hammered bronze of the walls. The wooden doors at the entrance to each stateroom contain finely carved abstract designs which are uniquely dissimilar from each other and different sets of Brimcolf numbers for labeling. Abandoning the dorm hall with its perfect symmetry, they enter into an expansive darker zone filled with the remnants of the clock tower and qwitsuls. Corroded gears and other clockwork mechanisms border them. Far below the security of the narrow path they're striding along, Phoebe can see more evidence of the airship's former occupation on the walls and floor. As several yuets pass by them in the opposing direction, Phoebe feels a wave of wonder sweep over her. She has never been fenced in by such a gargantuan, well-connected assortment of clockworks. Phoebe is captivated by the gyrating motions of the airship parts, blowing the qwitsuls around in circular motions. Even Mysty is constantly staring up at the perfectly connected mechanisms spinning around nonstop. Phoebe would hate to envision what would happen if someone jumped off the path only to end up being caught up between the mechanisms down below. Distracted by the revolving motions of the machinery, she inadvertently steps on Hilmina's tail. Hilmina yelps just like Phoebe would upon witnessing a spider. Phoebe and her kitten jump in surprise, their attention finally drawn away from the hypnotic gears. They stare down at Phoebe's foot squishing Hilmina's tail. Feeling extremely clumsy, Phoebe lifts her foot and gives Hilmina an apologetic look.

"Please be careful Qelphy," Hilmina says, sighing with annoyance.

"Sorry."

As they advance down the pathway, Phoebe, still mesmerized by the whirling gears, tries to maintain a safe distance between herself and Hilmina's drooping tail. Finally reaching the end of the mechanical chamber, they find themselves stopped in front of a sealed wooden door.

Hilmina opens the door and they walk out onto a steel outdoor deck, rimmed with steel guardrails. Phoebe halts at the bannister, staring out at the night skies of Yuetsion. The shining moons and qwitsul streams appear to shimmer with an otherworldly glow. The airship just barely manages to float at a high enough altitude to make it over the massive crystal mountains. Each crystalline mountain from its bottommost to its peak glows in a unique colour indicating the minerals making up their natural colour shades. The dreamlike vision helps to relieve her fearfulness, but only to a certain extent. Gazing over at the airship's sides, Phoebe can see most of the remaining portions of the clock tower have broken away. The airship now truly seems like an actual dirigible. She estimates the length of it to be around one-hundred metres! Awestruck by the advanced technology, Phoebe glances up at the three colossal propellers circling above the airship, gusting the qwitsuls around above. Along with the two propellers at the front and the ones further back, it makes a total of six propellers keeping them afloat. She gazes to her right and left, spotting holes in the outer walls of the airship, sucking in bright, powerful qwitsuls and dimmer, powerless qwitsuls flowing out through the airship walls downwards, heading towards the ground to be regenerated. *Wow, the machinery here really is qwitsul powered!*

"Impressive airship, don't you think?" Hilmina asks, snapping Phoebe out of her trance.

"Huh? Uh…" Phoebe nods in agreement and looks down at Mysty who's staring up at her impatiently. She turns curiously back to look at Hilmina. "Why was the clock tower…an airship in disguise?"

"Oh, that's because during times such as the Galprem War and the Kendent War," Hilmina says, "the yuets secretly built hidden airships within most of the towers and castles as a sneaky way of escaping from sudden enemy ambushes. Cernin managed to discover the code that uncovered this airship in one of his many books. It was my job to decode it by using my harp to move the clock hands. Of course there are switches that are also capable of moving them easily, but my harp speeds up the process."

Phoebe nods in fascination, wanting to ask Hilmina about her skills on her harp, but thoughts of Xeffizens concern her more and she finds herself prevented from any additional questions.

"Come along Qelphy. We shouldn't be far from an available room."

Hilmina leads Phoebe and Mysty back inside the airship into a different dorm filled hall, which is quite similar to the first one they had traveled through. They pass by many rooms until they finally come to an open door numbered 287. Hilmina peeks inside the unoccupied room and happily snaps her fingers.

"Perfect! An available room near Yorgo's and mine," Hilmina says, pointing at a door, three rooms to the left from them, numbered 290. "With this room, you can easily come to us for any help. Do you like it?"

Phoebe and Mysty wander in, taking in the comforting appearance. The bedroom is about the same size as her bedroom at home. It has enough space for one navy blue bed, a rectangular mirror sitting on a wooden desk with a wooden chair and a glimmering purple crystal lamp. Mysty playfully jumps around on the bed, making them chuckle.

"It's really nice," Phoebe says.

"I'm glad it's to your liking," Hilmina says. "By the way, if the qwitsuls' glow is too bothersome for your eyes to sleep in, there should be a sleeping mask within one of those drawers."

Phoebe walks over to the dresser and opens one of its drawers, finding a couple black cloth sleeping masks. "Oh, ace, thanks." *I prefer sleeping in pitch blackness after all.*

"So like I said before, if you need something or need to tell us anything, just ask anyone for Cernin, Hezkale, Yorgo or myself. We'll gladly help you."

"Thank you," Phoebe says. From their very first encounter, she has relished Hilmina's sympathetic presence.

"You're welcome, now you'd better get some sleep."

"Hilmina?"

"Yes?"

"What's…going to happen now, now that the…Xeff-Xeffizens know about me?" Phoebe asks, uneasily folding her hands.

Hilmina stares at her solemnly and kneels down. "No matter what happens, we will never let the Xeffizens lay a finger on you. No Xeffizen is going to mess with you, me or any of us." She stands back up, gazing out the window, straightening her shoulders in an attempt to appear more aggressive. "No Xeffizen, especially Wazure, I'll make sure of that."

Phoebe is surprised by Hilmina's abrupt serious, aggressive tone when she mentioned Wazure. From the little she knows of her, it seems really out of character. *Sheesh, I figure lots of yuets would hate Wazure, but for Hilmina…it seems more personal.* "About Wazure…he couldn't handle my loud whistling. Are Xeffizens weak to loudness?"

"As far as I know, no. I'm sure only Wazure is weak to loudness."

"Oh…If only all Xeffizens couldn't handle my whistling. One more thing?"

"Yes Qelphy?"

"Do you think I'll ever get back home?"

Hilmina beams back at Phoebe, the aggressive tone leaving her voice. "Yes Qelphy. Even if the Vinston Scepter doesn't end up working for you or our quest fails in the end, we'll definitely make sure you return home safely."

Phoebe smiles, feeling a bit more calm. It's reassuring to know she still has a good chance of returning to her home on Earth.

"Thank you very much," Phoebe says, as she sets her hand on Mysty's head and caresses it gently.

"You're very welcome." Hilmina walks out the door and smiles once more. "Goodnight Qelphy."

Hilmina softly closes the door, shutting out the light from the hall and leaving the lamps as the only remaining source of light in the room. Phoebe crawls onto the bed and sits up on her knees. She gazes out the window and sighs. After everything she's gone through, she knows she'll never be able to get a proper sleep. Any effort to do so would only bring up visions of what she had witnessed and leave her speculating about what she may come across in the future. She's also left with the realization of how much her family would be crying out for her. She can live with her fear, but at the same time she has never abandoned her desire to get back to her world and reunite with her family. As she places her hand onto her glowing amethyst necklace, the love of her family seeps out from inside of it.

"Mom and Dad have always told me that even a speck of hope can take anyone a long way." Mysty meows up at her questioningly. "Mysty, I have a feeling…that my speck of hope…is the fact that I'm still alive...with yuets on my side."

Phoebe lifts Mysty up, allowing her to stare out the window. A flock of a dozen gigantic shimmering, glowing feathered, hummingbird-like mincies lit by the qwitsuls zoom freely through the sky. Looping through the air, it appears as if they're leaving temporary shiny, multi-coloured trails behind them. Phoebe is flabbergasted by their company and the light shows their vibrating wings produce. The feathery fireflies skyrocket away, magically painting the nocturnal firmament. As the airship sails through the skies and the mincies coast in the distance, she feels her gaze drawn to the enchanting scenery passing by.

TO BE CONTINUED:

Stay tuned on http://jtldimension.weebly.com/ for any updates, including the release of:

Reflection

Book 2 — The Vinston Scepter

Jordan T. Lefaivre

Author's Acknowledgements, Author's Gratitude and Information About the Author Below:

Reflection Book 1: The Uishanole Acknowledgements

I would like to thank Marjorie Nielson, a good friend and former tutor of mine, for being a consistent and reliable editor for the Reflection novels.

Also, I thank the Killer Covers company for illustrating such a phenomenal front cover for Reflection Book 1. For anyone who wants amazing front covers for their books, here's the company's website's web link: https://killercovers.com/

I thank Will Johnson very much for being a helpful writing mentor and editor for Reflection Book 1 and for interviewing me to help the Reflection series get known before it got published. His internet name is Literary Goon 2.0. Here's his website's web link: http://literarygoon.tumblr.com/

I greatly thank my mom and dad, Joelle and Leighton, for all of the help and support they've given me to help me accomplish getting Reflection Book 1 published and will continue to give me to get the rest of the series published.

I thank Christine Pike for convincing me to write the Reflection series as novels instead of screenplays, which helped allow me to expand and be much more flexible with the Reflection series.

I would also like to thank all my ABA (Applied Behaviour Analysis) interventionists/tutors, Educational Assistants and teachers who helped me to improve many areas of my life, which also helped me write the Reflection series.

I also thank every person and company very much that promotes the Reflection series.

Most of all, God is the one who gifted me with the talents I have and I prayed to Him to help me write, edit and publish the Reflection series. Therefore, He deserves all the credit for the Reflection novel series.

Gratitude Towards Every Reader

To all those who choose to read the Reflection novel series, I truly thank you all so very much for the interest, time and support you give me and the series.

About the Author

I am Jordan Thomas Lefaivre and I'm a twenty-three-year-old with high-functioning autism. I'm an aspiring young fantasy author, who's been doing creative writing since age fourteen. I live with my parents and sister in Canada. I've been working on a five novel fantasy/adventure/sci-fi series called Reflection for around five years now. I, being diagnosed with autism since I was three, made sure Phoebe's autism is realistic and is well-mixed into the whole series. I'm very visual and I'm able to put my ideas into compelling stories.

My parents had me do ABA Therapy (Applied Behavioural Analysis) from the ages four to eighteen. It tremendously helped me with my learning and helped me become the person I am today.

I started my writing career by getting involved with acting in plays through the Creative Outlet organization. I then evolved into screenplay writing for a couple of years from being motivated to bring back traditional 2D hand-drawn animated movies, which I so miss. With my screenplays and previous stories not living up to my full satisfaction, a friend suggested to me to write my current story as a novel instead because novels get accepted easier than screenplays and there is more freedom in novel writing. I then moved into novel writing.

I am a Christian believer and I thank our Heavenly Father for keeping my life focused and for all His blessings. I would not be able to do the things that I can do without His helping hand. "Thank-you Father".

I am a graduate of the Booming Ground Program at the University of British Columbia.

My goal is to give readers a look into an original fantastical new world populated by original outer worldly characters. My aim is to spread great morals and autism awareness and understanding to all readers throughout the world by making Phoebe's character authentic.

If anyone wants to know more information about me, you can find it at this website here: https://jtldimension.weebly.com/

Made in the USA
San Bernardino, CA
06 February 2018